Francis Henry Underwood, William Goold

Henry Wadsworth Longfellow

A Bibliographic Sketch

Francis Henry Underwood, William Goold

Henry Wadsworth Longfellow
A Bibliographic Sketch

ISBN/EAN: 9783744652445

Printed in Europe, USA, Canada, Australia, Japan

Cover: Foto ©Raphael Reischuk / pixelio.de

More available books at **www.hansebooks.com**

HENRY WADSWORTH LONGFELLOW

A Biographical Sketch

BY

FRANCIS H. UNDERWOOD

AUTHOR OF HANDBOOKS OF ENGLISH LITERATURE, A BIOGRAPHICAL
SKETCH OF JAMES RUSSELL LOWELL,
ETC. ETC.

BOSTON
JAMES R. OSGOOD AND COMPANY
1882

UNIVERSITY PRESS:
JOHN WILSON AND SON, CAMBRIDGE.

PREFACE.

As it is known that the family of the deceased poet intend to publish a full account of his life, including his correspondence, which must be extensive and valuable, it is proper that a brief statement should be made as to the origin and status of this Biographical Sketch.

While Mr. Longfellow was in his usual health, somewhat more than a year ago, he kindly undertook the task of looking over my Sketch of James Russell Lowell. I had asked him to do this friendly service for me, and for Mr. Lowell, who could not be conveniently consulted. I have still the proof-sheets with annotations in his well-known hand. He praised the work; and, with the simple frankness of Priscilla in his Puritan romance, he intimated that he would be pleased to have one written of himself in a similar spirit. Up to that time I had not intended to undertake such a labor; his works were so many, and his fame so widely diffused, that I felt a sincere diffidence in approaching the subject. But, encouraged by his approbation, I began collecting materials, and making such studies as I could of his separate works. Being engaged in business to which I have been, and still am, bound to devote the most of my time, the work proceeded slowly. I did not imagine that the end was near, and supposed I should still have time to carry out my plans with care. Only a fortnight before his death I spent an evening in his library, and submitted to him my notes and data; I intended to go again within a few days, but soon learned that he was seriously ill. His death soon followed.

Having spent nearly all my spare time for a year in preparation, it appeared proper to complete the work as soon as it could be done.   Under these circumstances there has been less time to give completeness and finish than I could have desired.

It should be added, that I resided in Cambridge from 1854 to 1859, and enjoyed the friendship and often the invaluable converse of Longfellow and Lowell; and, as I was the projector of the Atlantic Monthly, and had been the means of gathering the eminent literary men who made it renowned, I was for the first two years a constant attendant at the monthly dinners hereinafter mentioned, and so came to have a personal knowledge of the great writers of our State and time.   And I have felt that it was something very like a duty for me to put on paper, before age should overtake me, my early impressions of that remarkable group of men, now sadly broken.

The Sketch of Lowell has been published; but it will be enlarged as soon as opportunity offers.   The Sketch of Longfellow is herewith presented.   Similar sketches of Whittier, Holmes, and Emerson will follow as speedily as circumstances allow.

Thanks are due to many persons for valuable aid. I must mention the services of Peter Thacher, Esq., William Winter, the poet, Charles Lanman, author and artist, H. W. Bryant, Librarian of the Maine Historical Society, Professor Charles Eliot Norton, Wm. P. P. Longfellow, Esq., nephew of the poet; and I must especially thank the family of the poet for the loan of Mr. Lanman's picture and the historic inkstands, and for furnishing the manuscript lines of which a fac-simile has been made.

FRANCIS H. UNDERWOOD.

Boston, April 27, 1882.

CONTENTS.

APPENDIX.

HENRY WADSWORTH LONGFELLOW

A Biography

HENRY WADSWORTH LONGFELLOW.

A BIOGRAPHICAL SKETCH.

A FRUITFUL literary life which has extended
over fifty years is necessarily an object of respectful interest and admiration. The labors
of most writers fall within the limits of a
generation, — a third of a century; their creative power seldom outlasts the ideas and
fashions among which they have grown up.
In fifty years there is time for a poet to have
seen, in his early days the decline of an old
school, in his manhood the rise and triumph of
a new one, and in his age the signs of change
and the dim forms of coming ideals in art.

Longfellow's first poems were written almost sixty years ago. Robert Southey was
then the English Laureate, who as a poet is

now wholly neglected and almost forgotten. Keats, Shelley, and Byron had only recently passed away; Scott, Wordsworth, Moore, Coleridge, Campbell, Hood, Landor, and Leigh Hunt were still living; Tennyson and Browning were soon to appear; and these, with their immediate predecessors, were to make the nineteenth century hardly less illustrious than the Elizabethan age.

It had been settled that rhymed argument or eloquence, such as prevailed in the eighteenth century, however compact, witty, and musical, is not necessarily poetry. Pope might still be called a poet, but his germinating influence had ceased. The formal heroics were obsolete, except that, like other departing fashions, they lingered in provincial districts. Poetry in England was occupied with noble themes, and had become once more thought etherealized.

The attention of the British is rarely turned upon their colonies, except as fields for trade, and as places for bettering the fortunes of younger sons. Their calm conceit of superiority has long been remarked; and one may be sure that the writers of the United States are in no danger of being spoiled by English flattery.

Fifty years ago the British had heard of Dr. Franklin; they had read the Declaration of Independence (at least their statesmen had); Washington Irving with his Sketch Book had made a pleasant ripple in London society; theologians had heard of Jonathan Edwards; and that was about all. Some few persons, curious in the literary annals of an obscure people, may have read the "Thanatopsis" in the North American Review; but the notion of the existence of American literature, especially of American poetry, would have caused a derisive roar from Aberdeen to Portsmouth.[1]

And the literature of the United States

---

[1] If the reader desires to see specimens of mingled ignorance and prejudice, he will find them in the articles upon American literature in the Encyclopædia Britannica.

fifty years ago, it must be confessed, existed largely in promise. Irving was favorably known on both shores of the Atlantic. Cooper had written "The Spy," and was famous. Joseph Rodman Drake's "Culprit Fay," a pleasing performance for a youth, was thought to be a happy portent. Fitz-Greene Halleck, Robert C. Sands, and Gulian C. Verplanck were in the flush of youth and hope. Bryant had made a noble beginning, and the elevated thought and sure movement of his verse prognosticated higher renown. Emerson, the most original of English-speaking men in this century, was preaching at the North End of Boston. So far as the public knew, there was no hint of his poetry or of the great Essays yet. Prescott was reading and meditating for his brilliant histories. Bancroft was then a politician, and had not entered upon his great work. Dr. Palfrey was discoursing upon the Old Testament at the Theological School of Cambridge. Willis, born in the same year with Longfellow, was trying his 'prentice hand in verse, and was to become for the next twenty years the most popular, as he was the most versatile, of the light-armed corps of writers. Dana, after a few tantalizing successes, became

"Involved in a paulo-post-future of song."

Sprague had recited his fine Shakespeare and Centennial Odes, and settled back into his comfortable and honorable banker's chair. John Pierpont had admirers; so had John Neal and Mrs. Sigourney. Edgar A. Poe was just becoming known; his first verses were published in 1829. The literary world, and Longfellow in particular, were to hear much of him in the following twenty years. Hawthorne, who was Longfellow's college classmate, published his first volume later, in 1837, and was truly, as he himself said, "the obscurest man of letters in America."

On the whole, we may say that the works which have a reasonable chance to live, written previous to Longfellow's beginning, are very few, and they are not in the department of poetry. The loyalty and zeal of Dr. Griswold, and the exhaustive labors of the brothers Duyckinck, have preserved for us a mass of details which are copious materials for literary history, but of which very little can be considered as belonging to our national literature. For oblivion has already settled down upon the greater part of the names and the works held in honor fifty years ago; and to look back upon Griswold's " Poets and Poetry of America" is like taking a distant view of Mount Auburn Cemetery by moonlight.

The public taste half a century ago was unformed. The public taste is far from infallible now; but the elders know that there has been a wide-spread change. It is seen in many apparently trivial things. The popular poetry fifty years ago was matched by the cheap and gaudy colored lithographs, and by the plaster images of Italian pedlers, both of which forms of "art" were as pervasive as the colors of the national flag. There was no literary standard. The average editor thought more of the "scream of the American eagle" than of any canon of taste. There were no canons of taste or laws of criticism. Any sentiment in a musical flow of words, with sparkles of high-colored adjectives, was a poem. And as for poets capable of such verses, in the slang of the frontiers "the woods were full of them."

Few editors and fewer readers were liberally educated. In the public schools the reading was largely from eighteenth-century authors, while the notions of rhetoric and criticism were derived from Blair or Lord Kaimes, pedants who never knew the idioms of English. So, between old-fashioned professors who taught what was gone by, and the fluent, self-confident apostles of jingle and glitter (whose field was in milliners' magazines and red-morocco annuals), the student, if there were one, had no secure middle ground.

It would require the space of a volume to show the influences which have been at work since 1830 to build up our literature, or rather to lay a foundation for it, and to connect it with our social and political life. The period is that of our greatest expansion in population, wealth, and power, of the greatest improvements in the arts, of the greatest diffusion of intelligence, and the one in which the bulk of American literature has been produced. All benign influences have acted in concert. To a public like that of 1830 the best productions of our day would have been enigmatical or ridiculous. The education of that public, so far as it has gone, has been an enormous work, for which every moral as well as material force has been employed. Schoolmasters, engineers, preachers, reformers, philosophers, inventors, printers, — these with the editors and authors have been slowly raising the level of thought and achievement, — building, as it were, under a whole people a foundation like that of Persepolis, on which the rising structure of our letters and art is to stand. Every new era brings new powers and advantages; but it is hardly possible that there will ever be a time in which the vast work of our century will be eclipsed.

It must be considered a good fortune for Longfellow to have been born at a period when national prosperity was fairly begun, to have grown with his country's growth, to have reached maturity when its literature was for the first time reckoned as a power, and to have attained to serene old age at a time when the whole reunited republic regarded him with honor and pride. The public life of no other American author has covered such a span; the period of no other has so many fortunate incidents; the fame of no other is so universal among all classes of men.

The chief honors in American letters thus

far have been gained by poets. In history, science, and criticism, with a few brilliant exceptions, we have produced little to be compared with the works of Englishmen. The influences of great universities and the cultivation and inherited tastes of the leading classes (such as exist in England) are almost wholly wanting in America. The power of such a literary centre as London is almost solar. There is no such gravitation in our western hemisphere. At the first thought it might appear that poets, whose genius is inborn, do not need the stimulus of learned society, and are not aided by breathing a literary atmosphere. But though the poet's original impulse comes from the Creator, and that which is vital in his verse is due to no teaching, yet his taste, his skill and mastery, are largely affected by his surroundings, and, unless he is a man of self-centred power, by the public sympathy, or the want of it.

Poets of the first order are so rare that they

cannot be reckoned in any Buckle's system of averages. England has produced two, Shakespeare and Milton. Poets of the second order, such as Chaucer, Spenser, Byron, Coleridge, Keats, Shelley, Wordsworth, and Dryden, are more evenly distributed among the generations. Leaving Robert Browning out of the account (for the present), we find among living English poets only one pre-eminent, the Laureate Tennyson. It is probably no more than just to assign his rank as being the first since Milton. At the same time there are living in America Emerson, Lowell, Holmes, and Whittier; and these, with Longfellow and Bryant, lately deceased, appear to educated Americans superior severally in genius and in accomplishment to any living English poet, save Tennyson.[1]

[1] This is a plain statement of an indubitable truth; and in view of the invincible ignorance of British reviewers and cyclopædists it appears necessary for an American writer once in a while to publish concisely his articles of belief. We are English in blood, not aliens, and English literature and thought are ours. "If you prick us, do we not bleed?—if you tickle us, do we not laugh?"

THE LONGFELLOW FAMILY.

The old town of Newbury, in the north-eastern part of Massachusetts, has an interesting history. It was the birthplace of an unusual number of intellectual and eminent men. So many poets, jurists, preachers, mathematicians and college professors have sprung from the primitive stock, that the list of "freemen" embraces the names of the best known families in the Commonwealth.[1] Among them are Cushing, Danà, Emerson, Felton, Gould, Greenleaf, Hale, Jackson, Lunt, Longfellow, Lowell, Noyes, Pierce, Sewall, Story, Whipple, Whittier, and Woods. Each generation appears also to have had a full share of the intellectual training which was possible at the time. No less than 308 graduates of Harvard College (from 1642 to 1845) were born in Newbury. Considering the early poverty, the trials attending the

[1] See Joshua Coffin's unique and excellent History of Newbury.

settlement of a new country, and the hostilities with Indians, French, and the mother country, this is a remarkable record.

William Longfellow, who was born in 1651, and probably in Hosforth, near Leeds, in Yorkshire, came to this country in 1676, settled in Newbury, and, in November, 1678, married Ann Sewall, sister of the well-known Chief Justice. The commonly accepted account is that he came from Hampshire; but this is evidently an error. Samuel Sewall, writing to his brother Stephen, at Bishop-Stoke, Hampshire, October 24, 1680, says: —

" Bro. Longfellow's Father, Willm Longfellow lives at Hosforth, near Leeds in Yorkshire. Tell him Bro. has a son W^m a fine likely child, a very good piece of Land, & greatly wants a little stock to manage it." [1]

It is known that the father was alive in August, 1687, but probably died in the autumn, as the son went to England in No-

[1] N. E. Hist. and Genealog. Register, Vol. XXIV. No. 2, April, 1870.

vember or December of that year to get his patrimony.

The residence of William Longfellow was in the Byfield parish of Newbury. "The location of the house is unsurpassed. It is situated on a sightly eminence at the very head of tide water on the river Parker, the sparkle of whose waters, as they go tumbling over the falls, adds a picturesqueness to the natural beauty of the scenery that lies spread on either hand. . . . . Nature was lavish here, and young Longfellow, appreciating it all, erected the house to which he took his young bride. It still stands, though two centuries and more have passed since its oaken frame was put together. It has not been occupied for twenty odd years, and of course is in a dilapidated condition. The large chimney was taken down years ago," — to the poet's great regret, — "and a part of the house itself has been removed."[1]   The picture of

<hr>

[1] Letter of Horace F. Longfellow to the Brunswick Telegraph, March 10, 1882.

THE HOUSE AT NEWBURY.

the house and surroundings was painted by Charles Lanman, and presented to the poet, by whose favor it was copied.

As ensign of the Newbury company, the first American Longfellow had a part in the disastrous expedition against Quebec under command of Sir William Phipps. The force, consisting of 2,200 soldiers, set sail in thirty-two vessels from Boston, August 9, 1690. The attempt to capture the stronghold failed, and the expedition was abandoned. On the return voyage a violent storm in the Gulf of St. Lawrence scattered the fleet, and one of the vessels, containing the Newbury company, was wrecked on the island of Anticosti. William Longfellow and nine others were drowned.[1]

Stephen Longfellow, son of the first settler William, was born in 1685. He was the " village blacksmith " and ensign in the militia of the town. He married Abigail Thompson, daughter of a clergyman in Marshfield; and

---

[1] Sewall's Diary, Nov. 21, 1690, Vol. I. p. 335.

the position of an "elder" in a theocracy like the Massachusetts Colony was a strong guaranty for the respectability of his son-in-law. His fifth son, Stephen, was born at the old homestead, February 7, 1723, and was graduated at Harvard College in 1742.   He lived for a short time at York, and in 1745 was invited to Portland (then a part of Falmouth) to take charge of the grammar school.[1]   A curious item is preserved as to his salary.   It was fixed by the town at £50 for the first year, besides 18*s.* 6*d.* tuition to be paid by each scholar.   The second year his salary was raised to £200.   The records of the time attest that he was probably one of the most widely known and respected citizens of the District of Maine.   For nearly thirty years he held office, as clerk of the town and parish, Register of Probate, and Clerk of the Judicial Court.   His handwriting was fair and regular, and his habits of mind methodical and clerkly.   This peculiarity of beauti-

[1] This appears in the Diary of Rev. Thomas Smith.

ful penmanship has continued in the family to this day. Tradition has it that he was a bright and entertaining companion, noted for sallies of wit and for inexhaustible good humor. A note in the diary of the Rev. Thomas Smith records the fact that Longfellow once accompanied him to an ordination, and was so lively (in spite of the solemnity of the occasion) that, says the good parson, "I fear we somewhat passed the bounds of decorum."

This clerical Longfellow married Tabitha Bragdon, of York, in 1749. A son was born in 1750, August 3, and was duly christened Stephen. At the age of twenty-three this Stephen was married to Patience Young of York. He lived at Gorham (whither also his father came afterwards), and was a surveyor by profession. He held many public offices, and was Judge of the Common Pleas from 1797 to 1811. Persons still living remember him as he drove into Portland "in an old square-topped chaise." "He was a fine-look-

ing gentleman, with the bearing of the old
school, erect, portly, rather taller than the
average, with a strongly marked face, and his
hair tied behind in a club with a black ribbon. To the close of his life he wore the old
style of dress, — knee breeches, a long waistcoat, and white top-boots. He was a man of
sterling qualities of mind and heart, — sterling integrity, and sound common sense."[1]

Falmouth, an important place on account of
its noble harbor, was bombarded by a British fleet under command of Captain Henry
Mowatt, October 18, 1775. This was in return for the indignity of an arrest endured
by Moffatt when ashore. Over four hundred
buildings were burned, and the greater number of citizens were driven to the interior.
The Longfellow family removed to Gorham,
a few miles west, and continued to reside
there. Stephen, the Clerk of Court, died
there in 1790. His son, the Judge, died
there in 1824.

[1] Rev. H. S. Burrage, Portland Advertiser, Feb. 28, 1882.

Stephen Longfellow, father of the poet, was born in Gorham, March 23, 1776. At the age of eighteen he entered Harvard College, and was graduated with honor in 1798. His rank is attested by his being chosen a member of the Phi Beta Kappa Society.

The descriptions of his person and manners, and of the qualities of his mind and heart, read as if they had been written for the poet himself.[1]

His classmate, Humphrey Devereux, of Salem, says: "On entering college, Longfellow (Stephen) was in advance in years of many of us, and his mind and judgment, of course, more matured. He had a well balanced mind, no part so prominent as to overshadow the rest. . . . . In his temperament, he was bright and cheerful, and engaged freely in the social pleasures of friendly meetings and literary associations. His manners then as in later life were courteous,

---

[1] "The Law, Courts, and Lawyers of Maine," by William Willis.

polished, and simple, springing from a native politeness or a generous, manly feeling. He was born a gentleman, and was a general favorite of his class."

The illustrious Dr. Channing says: "I never knew a man more free from everything offensive to good taste or good feeling; even to his dress and personal appearance, all about him was attractive. . . . . He was evidently a well-bred gentleman when he left the paternal mansion for the University. He seemed to breathe an atmosphere of purity as his natural element, while his bright intelligence, buoyant spirits, and social warmth diffused a sunshine of joy that made his presence always gladsome."

His portrait (in Willis's volume) is that of a bright, clear-minded, courteous, and refined gentleman. He studied law in Portland, in the office of Salmon Chase, an eminent advocate, uncle of Salmon Portland Chase, afterwards Secretary of the Treasury in the Cabinet of Abraham Lincoln, and Chief Justice of the United States Supreme Court. He attained a very high rank at the bar, as well as an influential position among his fellow-citizens. In the year 1814 he was sent as a delegate to the famous Hartford Convention of Federalists. In 1822 he was elected a member of Congress, and served with Webster, Clay, Randolph, Buchanan, and other distinguished men. But he did not accept a renomination; public life had no charm for him, and he gladly returned to his profession. In 1824, as the leading citizen, he welcomed Lafayette to Portland, and was honored by an exquisitely graceful reply. He continued to devote himself to his legal business, to the interests of Bowdoin College, of which he was one of the Trustees, and to the Maine Historical Society, of which he was an active and efficient member.

He was married, January 1, 1804, to Zilpah, daughter of General Peleg Wadsworth, who was a prominent officer in the war of independence. General Wadsworth was a man of high character and of eminent ability. It would be impossible here to give even the most cursory sketch of his long and active life.[1] It should be mentioned, however, that he was descended from the Pilgrims of Plymouth, Mass., five of his ancestors, including Elder Brewster and John Alden, having been passengers in the first memorable voyage of the Mayflower. The genealogy of the Wadsworths, and the line of descent from John Alden may be seen in the Appendix.

The ancestry of the family of the poet's mother is interesting on account of the connection with the well-known tradition of Captain Miles Standish's vicarious courtship. She was connected by two different lines to that Priscilla Mullen whose significant answer, " Why don't you speak for yourself, John ? " has been preserved in the beautiful romance of her descendant. Zilpah Wads-

[1] See his Memoir in the Appendix, by the Hon. William Goold, of Windham, Me.

LONGFELLOW'S BIRTHPLACE, PORTLAND.

worth was born in Duxbury, Mass., Jan. 6, 1788, while her father was in the Revolutionary army. All accounts tend to show that she was a superior woman, possessed of her full share of the hereditary bravery and honorable qualities which marked her father and her gallant brothers. At the close of the war her father and family removed to Maine, and lived partly in Portland and partly in the town of Hiram, then called Wadsworth's Grant, the name of a large tract of land bought by the General from the State of Massachusetts.

Mr. Longfellow lived for the first year after his marriage in the house built by his wife's father, now known as the Longfellow house. It stands upon Congress Street, adjoining the Preble House. It happened in the autumn of 1806 that a sister, Mrs. Stephenson, invited Mr. Longfellow and wife to pass the winter in her house, on account of the absence of her husband in the West Indies. The Stephenson house, a large, square wooden structure, is still standing at the corner of Fore and Hancock Streets. It was during the temporary residence of the family at this house that the poet was born. His name was given in remembrance of his mother's brother, Henry Wadsworth, a brilliant young naval officer, who fell in the attack upon Tripoli in 1804.

Not long after, General Wadsworth removed to his estate in Hiram; and from that time the family of Stephen Longfellow continued to occupy the General's house.

Mr. Longfellow, the poet's father, lived in happiness with the wife of his youth for more than forty-five years. There were born to them four sons and four daughters. Stephen, the eldest, the poet's classmate in college, died in 1850. Alexander Wadsworth Longfellow is still living in Portland. The Rev. Samuel Longfellow is an esteemed clergyman in Germantown, near Philadelphia, and is the author of numerous admirable poems. Elizabeth Wadsworth Longfellow died in 1829, and Ellen Longfellow in 1834. Two daughters survive, Mrs. Anne Longfellow Pierce, of Portland, and Mrs. Mary Longfellow Greenleaf, of Cambridge, Mass. The father died, August 3, 1849, at the age of seventy-four. The poet, who was the second son, was born in Portland, February 27, 1807.

It will be seen that the poet inherited the best blood of the two early colonies, Pilgrim and Puritan; and that his place in the line of descent was where the best qualities of both came to maturity. The rise of families from obscurity, the increase of intellectual power (following wise marriages) generation by generation, and the progressive refinement of taste and feeling, until the accumulation forces the blossom of genius in the person of some fortunate descendant, is a most interesting study. The problem is to continue the culture without tending to loss of power, and without sacrificing the individuality.

After tracing the lines of descent with as

much care as is possible, a biographer must still feel that he is far from the mystery of the genesis of genius. The Longfellows for generations were tall and vigorous men, with the instincts and training of soldiers; the Wadsworths had their virtues and their heroic bravery; but never before this fortunate conjunction (so far as we know) was there in either family a gleam of the poetic faculty. After all that has been written upon heredity, it remains true, we think, that genius is a miracle. The sober and practical abilities commonly grouped under the name of talent are transmissible. Good bodies, solid characters, courage, good sense, and capacity for affairs, may be predicted with something like certainty in well-descended families; but no one can say that at such a point there will be born the creator of a Hamlet, an Endymion, a Childe Harold, an Evangeline, or a Sir Launfal. In fact, it is almost certain that there are not half a dozen instances in all history of two men of unquestioned genius who bear to each other the relation of father and son. Poets have, as a rule, left few inheritors of their blood, and those have seldom been singers by impulse.

Though nothing that is ultimately perfect is produced without labor, yet in the case of a man of genius, whether poet, sculptor, or painter, that which distinguishes him is the almost unconscious development of creative power. He does not toil for an image of beauty; it comes to him. As Longfellow observed, " What we call miracles and wonders of art are not so to him who created them; for they were created by the natural movements of his own great soul. Statues, paintings, churches, poems, are but shadows of himself, — shadows in marble, colors, stone, words. He feels and recognizes their beauty; but he thought these thoughts and produced these things as easily as inferior minds do thoughts and things inferior."

In the Longfellow family the foundations were laid two centuries ago. Each father strove to place his son in a higher position than he himself had held. Each was faithful to his appointed task, and to the duty which was nearest. The long wars with the French and Indians, and afterwards with England, allowed no time for any but practical studies. Character then as now counted for more than accomplishment. The axe, the spade, and the musket were more familiar to early Longfellows than the pen. It was not until peace came, and plenty followed, and the labors of the farmer, the advocate, and the judge had brought prosperity and affluence and the right of leisure into the family, that there was a possibility of " The Psalm of Life," or " The Footsteps of Angels."

In the sketch of Lowell it was shown that poetry was incompatible with early Puritanism. It is needless here to dwell upon the barrenness of the first century of our history, or to detail the causes which so long prevented the development of literature and art. For half a century after the peace with Great Britain there was a brooding time. Wounds were healed; laws were re-established; colleges were reopened and schools fostered; trade sprung up; ascetic views of life faded; provincial narrowness disappeared; and then came a revival or new birth of letters. In this fortunate time the poet Longfellow was born.

PORTLAND.[1]

Few cities upon the seaboard are so beautifully situated as Portland. The view to one coming up the harbor is something never to be forgotten. Cape Elizabeth stretches out on one hand like a gigantic wall, with a light-house at its southern extremity; and on the other are the many lovely islands of Casco Bay. The city rises from the water

[1] For this part of his work the author has made free use of the elaborate account by Edward H. Elwell, Esq., published in the Portland Advertiser, Feb. 28, 1882.

by easy and natural swells, and the *ensemble* is completed by the dome-like crowns of Munjoy and Bramhall Hills. Behind are natural forests, and a profusion of noble trees skirt the principal streets. This charming union of rural and urban beauty, as seen from the harbor, gives a delightful surprise to the incoming voyager. The Forest City is its very appropriate and picturesque name. Hints of this remembered beauty are to be seen in Longfellow's poem entitled "My Lost Youth."

> "I can see the shadowy lines of its trees,
>   And catch, in sudden gleams,
> The sheen of the far-surrounding seas,
> And islands that were the Hesperides
>   Of all my boyish dreams."

> "I can see the breezy dome of groves,
>   The shadows of Deering's Woods,"

In the latter part of the last century it was a fishing village, and was called Falmouth Neck. Its recovery was slow after its destruction by the British fleet; but in 1807,

THE LONGFELLOW HOUSE, PORTLAND.

VIERU
GHILAȘ

the year of Longfellow's birth, it had become a place of commercial importance.[1]

> "I remember the black wharves and the slips
>   And the sea-tides tossing free ;
> And Spanish sailors with bearded lips,
> And the beauty and mystery of the ships,
>   And the magic of the sea."

In 1812, during the war, defensive works were erected on the shore, and garrisons were established on Munjoy Hill. The impressions of that stirring time were never effaced. Longfellow's sonorous lines show how deeply his boyish mind was affected.

> " I remember the bulwarks by the shore,
>   And the fort upon the hill ;
> The sunrise gun with its hollow roar,
> The drum-beat repeated o'er and o'er,
>   And the bugle wild and shrill.
>   And the music of that old song
>   Throbs in my memory still :
> ' A boy's will is the wind's will,
> And the thoughts of youth are long, long thoughts.' "

[1] As an evidence of the business of Portland, it may be mentioned that in 1806, when its population was probably less than 7,000, the tonnage of its shipping was 39,000, and the duties collected amounted to $346,444.

Another tragic reminiscence was the sea-fight between the British brig Boxer and the United States brig Enterprise, which took place off the coast. The captains of both vessels were killed in the action, and were buried in the cemetery at the foot of Munjoy Hill. In the poem before quoted is this stanza: —

> "I remember the sea-fight far away,
>   How it thundered o'er the tide !
> And the dead captains, as they lay
> In their graves, o'erlooking the tranquil bay,
>   Where they in battle died.
>   And the sound of that mournful song
>   Goes through me with a thrill :
> 'A boy's will is the wind's will,
> And the thoughts of youth are long, long thoughts.'"

At the time of Longfellow's boyhood, the fashions of the Revolutionary period were just passing away. The speech of the people was homely, and inflected with the old Yankee accent. Cows were pastured on Munjoy Hill. There were few private carriages. A stage conveyed passengers to Boston; but much of the intercourse with other sea-coast towns was by sailing-vessels. When, afterwards, the young Longfellows went to college, they made the journey by coasters through Casco Bay to Harpswell. The two newspapers were published weekly. There was no theatre or other place of amusement, but West India rum was plentiful and in daily use. There were learned lawyers and clergymen, but it is not probable that there was much in the intellectual life of the town to favor the development of a poet.

In the towns near the sea-coast, from Newport to Portland, there was a great similarity in domestic architecture. A large number of the better class of the old houses have been torn down or rebuilt. In Boston and vicinity very few remain; although in Charlestown, Cambridge, Salem, Newburyport, Portsmouth, Exeter, Dover, and towns farther eastward, we can still behold the typical New England mansion. It is ample in size and stately in form. It is associated with reminiscences of ruffles, shoe-buckles, silver-topped canes, courtly manners, and hospitality. It is the house of the judge, the Continental general, the squire, the prosperous doctor of divinity or of medicine, or of the merchant whose ships have brought him spices, ivory, and gold dust from over sea. It is generally of three stories, the third being somewhat abridged; and the form is quadrangular, fifty feet on a side. Various extensions and out-buildings are in the rear, and sometimes on the sides. The front door opens into a wide hall, from which a grand stairway leads to the upper stories. The hall is wainscoted, and hung with rather stiff portraits. The stairway is broad and the steps are wide, giving an easy ascent to the landings. Twist-ed and carved balusters support the hand-rail, each one wrought separately in some quaint device. There are four large, square rooms on the ground floor, each with its open fireplace and elaborately carved mantel-piece. The walls are thick, like those of a fortalice, and the windows are recessed like embrasures. Those who are accustomed to the cardboard structures of our time, whether in the form of Italian villas, Swiss chalets, or white-pine Gothic, have a strange sensation in visiting these solid dwellings. There is an air of repose in them, an idea of amplitude and permanence. One feels that the builders must have been large-minded, serene men. A fashionable dwelling of fifteen feet front on the new land of the Back Bay in Boston furnishes a perfect antithesis. The ancient houses were well placed, in grounds of some extent, on the crest of a natural elevation, or near a grove, with broad, grassy lawns, bordered by elms and oaks, and dotted with firs and spruces, and with clumps of flowering shrubs. The distinguishing features of the old towns of New England are still these superb mansions. They are generally painted buff or cream-white, having green blinds and high and heavy chimneys; and in their picturesque situations and surroundings they give an almost poetical charm to the landscape.

Such is a general description of the houses in which Longfellow has lived: the Stephenson house and the Wadsworth-Longfellow house in Portland, and the Vassall-Craigie house in Cambridge.

It will be remembered that the poet's father was a highly successful and prosperous advocate, and that his maternal grandfather was possessed of an ample estate, and it is fair to presume that the boy had every advantage in his education which wealth and liberality could procure.

It should also be remembered that with the sensible men of the last generation the training of boys to habits of industry and obedience was not as now one of the lost arts. Unquestionably, the poet and his brothers and sisters had the strict and careful training which has been the making of so many honorable and useful men and women, in New England and elsewhere.

But on the other hand there were never kinder or more considerate parents than Stephen and Zilpah Longfellow.

BOYHOOD AND YOUTH.

At a very early age our poet attended a private school kept by Mrs. Fellows, and afterwards another kept by Mr. Nathaniel H. Carter. This master became afterwards Principal of the Portland Academy, and there Longfellow began to prepare for college. During the latter part of the time he was under the charge of Mr. Cushman, who succeeded Carter. Mr. Carter was a man of superior attainments, and wrote a volume of patriotic poems; though one wonders into what limbo of forgetfulness the volume has fallen. When he left Portland he went to New York and became editor of the Evening Post, afterwards Mr. Bryant's paper. At the age of fourteen Henry and his elder brother Stephen entered Bowdoin College, at Brunswick, not far east of Portland. For the first year he pursued his studies mainly at home.

He must have been a great reader as well as a thorough student, because in his earliest writings there is an evident wide acquaintance with English and other modern literatures. In fact, his was hardly a " boyhood," in the usual sense of the term. He enjoyed an occasional sail among the islands, and was a frequent visitor at the paternal home in Gorham and at the house of his grandfather Wadsworth. In these places, which are full of beautiful water-courses, woods, and meadows, he gained the intimate acquaintance with nature which is the indispensable training of a poet. From these rural scenes, and from the views of the countless green islands and the storm-beaten coast, he drew the inspiration which was to be as lasting as life.

But he does not appear to have had time, or perhaps inclination, for the common outdoor sports and pastimes of youth. Yacht-

THE "WADSWORTH" HOUSE, HIRAM, ME.

ing, hunting, fishing, and games were for such as did not propose to become learned at twenty. It is strange to think of a hearty, vigorous, and manly boy advancing to maturity without boyish adventures, peccadilloes, or accidents, and gliding into a professor's chair in a few years after leaving his mother's knee.

Among his classmates, besides his brother, were Hawthorne, John S. C. Abbott, Rev. George B. Cheever, Cilley, who was killed in a duel by Graves of Kentucky, and James W. Bradbury. His scholarship was evident from the beginning, and at graduation he stood second in a class numbering thirty-seven. He was appointed one of the orators, and was assigned the theme of "Chatterton"; but the Faculty was induced to change the theme proposed, and he delivered an oration on "American Literature."

How Longfellow looked at this period, as well as the impression he made upon his associates, may be seen in a recent letter from his classmate Bradbury to Peter Thacher, Esq.[1] The reference to Hawthorne, though perhaps gratuitous, is an interesting bit of literary history.

"AUGUSTA, January 13, 1882.

" DEAR SIR, ...

" My recollection is that he entered college a Sophomore,[2] and that I was examined with him to enter old Bowdoin in the same class. He was then quite young, with a slight, erect figure, a remarkably fair and delicate complexion, with the bloom of health, clear blue eyes, an intelligent and pleasing expression of countenance, and a good head covered with a profusion of rather light brown hair. He was an agreeable companion, kindly and social in his manner, rendering himself dear to his associates by his disposition and deportment. Pure in his tastes and morals, his character was without a stain. As a scholar, while indulging in general reading, and occasionally flirting with the Muses, he always came to the recitation-room so thoroughly prepared in his

---

[1] Mr. Thacher is a well-known lawyer of Boston, and his wife is the sister of the first wife of the poet.

[2] Only partially correct.

lessons that he placed himself in the front rank in the large and able class of 1825; and on graduating he received one of the three English orations assigned to that class for the Commencement exercises, — the English orations then and for more than thirty years afterward outranking the Latin in that College.

" In the recitation-room he was greatly superior to his subsequently illustrious classmate, Hawthorne, who often came so poorly prepared in his lessons that he was one of the twelve in a class of thirty-eight to whom no part was assigned at Commencement.

" Hawthorne (then spelt Hathorne) was in college a peculiar and rather remarkable young man, — shy, retiring, fond of general reading, busy with his own thoughts, and usually alone or with one or two of his special friends, Pierce (afterwards President), and Horatio Bridge of Augusta.

" It is a remarkable fact in Hawthorne's history as an author that, after he had left the manuscript for his first volume with Mr. Goodrich [1] for publication, Mr. Bridge had occasion to inquire why the issue of it was delayed, and was

---

[1] Samuel G. Goodrich, a well-known writer, with the pseudonym of Peter Parley.

told by Mr. Goodrich that, as the author was un-
known, he needed some guaranty against loss. Mr.
Bridge thereupon gave his guaranty, unknown to
Hawthorne.

"Had he been apprised of Mr. Goodrich's re-
fusal, with his sensitive nature, it is likely that he
would have withdrawn and burnt the manuscript,
and possibly the world would have lost the fruits
of his rare genius.

"Very truly yours,

"JAMES W. BRADBURY."

The venerable Professor Packard, who
was a member of the Faculty in the same
period, has written a short account of the
appearance of Longfellow as a student. This
is in a letter which is also addressed to Mr.
Thacher.

"BRUNSWICK, ME., January 12, 1882.

"MY DEAR SIR, —

"Your letter of yesterday has just been received.
In regard to Mr. Longfellow's appearance, &c. in
college, I have only a few distinct reminiscences.
I remember him as a light-haired, agreeable, well-
bred, and well-mannered youth. I judge that his

preferences were for classical studies, and whatever addressed the æsthetic element was largely developed in him at an early period. His poetic effusions attracted notice as the 'Poet's Corner' in Portland newspapers, and in college placed him in the highest rank of college poets. During a winter vacation I was visiting in Boston, and met Mr. Carter, then conducting the 'Literary Gazette,' who asked me whom we had in our college that wrote such fine poetry? It was Longfellow. He delivered the poem at the anniversary of the Peucinian Society, the same season. I cannot name it. Mr. J. S. C. Abbott, in his address to his class at their fiftieth anniversary, in 1875, related an incident which I had not known before; viz. that young Longfellow's translation of an Ode of Horace at the annual examination in his Sophomore year attracted the notice of Hon. Benjamin Orr, one of the committee of examination, and led him to think of him as a candidate for the new Professorship of Modern Languages then in contemplation.

"He did not have a poem at his graduation, because the rank of a poem was indefinite, and he was assigned one of the English orations, the highest class of appointments.

" You see that I have not much in detail to write concerning Mr. Longfellow ; but I have a distinct image of him in memory as he sat, in his Sophomore year, in the recitation-room, North Entry, Maine, middle back room. I regret to hear that he is in feeble health. I did not call upon him when I spent several days in Boston undergoing the dull process of sitting for my portrait, for my time was occupied, and moreover I avoid any increase of the interruptions such a man must experience every day.

"I am faithfully yours,

"A. S. PACKARD."

Longfellow's college themes were frequently skilful versions from Horace and other classic authors; and this fact, together with his uncommon maturity of mind and character, drew attention to him at an early period, and led subsequently to his appointment to the newly established chair of Modern Languages, for which Madame Bowdoin gave the foundation.

Professor Cleaveland, the eminent mineralogist, was a member of the Faculty at this time; and though their tastes and pursuits varied, it is believed that the elder, who was a very able and magnetic man, exercised a salutary influence upon the mind of the rising poet. Longfellow has commemorated the Professor in a fine sonnet.

WOOING THE MUSES.

Like all inspired poets, Longfellow began to write verses at an early age. The " Earlier Poems " in the collected edition are such as he thought worth preserving. It appears to us, however, that some of those which he rejected are quite equal to the ones he chose to acknowledge. With a pleasing quaintness he has prefaced the group thus: —

" These poems were written for the most part during my college life, and all of them before the age of nineteen. Some have found their way into schools, and seem to be successful. Others lead a vagabond and precarious existence in the corners·of newspapers; or have changed their names and run away to seek their fortunes beyond the sea. I say, with the Bishop of Avranches on a similar occasion: "I cannot be displeased to see these children of mine, which I have neglected, and almost exposed, brought from their wanderings in lanes and alleys, and safely lodged, in order to go forth into the world together in a more decorous garb.'"

These with a number of others were published in the United States Literary Gazette, conducted by Theophilus Parsons and James C. Carter.[1] The remuneration for them was small indeed. A short time before his death Mr. Longfellow told the author that on one occasion, in Boston, having received notice that the munificent sum of *thirteen dollars* had been placed to his credit, for two poems and a prose article, he declined to receive the money, but accepted instead a set of Chatterton's Works, which are still in his library. This was the day of small things in letters.

[1] Longfellow's contributions to this periodical have lately been collected and published in London. His poems not included in his complete works will be found, with dates, etc., in the Appendix.

The public-spirited writers for the North American Review at that time not only furnished their articles without pay, but often had to contribute to make up the losses of the printer.

It may also be said here that our poet got no pay from the Knickerbocker Magazine, though he was promised *five dollars* each for the " Psalm of Life " and " The Reaper and the Flowers." Almost every literary man in America had a similar experience with the last-named periodical. To be sure, Milton's traditionary five pounds for " Paradise Lost " was a more unconscionable bargain;[1] but in our day, when poets seldom receive less than from fifty to two hundred dollars for short poems, the thought of buying the immortal " Psalm of Life " for five dollars, and not paying for it either, appears preposterous.

---

[1] The current story is not true. See the account in Masson's Life of Milton, wherein it is shown that Milton and his family received altogether £28 for the poem.

Mr. Samuel Ward (in the New York World, March 25, 1882) says respecting "The Reaper and the Flowers": "I was greatly stirred by the dash of the verse and the symmetry of the series of pictures it so graphically presented. I took the poem and read it aloud, and I think that the poet's own opinion was confirmed by my enthusiastic rendering of the part. I carried it to New York, where, having shown it to the poet Halleck, and obtained a certificate from him of its surpassing lyric excellence, I sold it to Mr. Lewis Gaylord Clarke, of the Knickerbocker Magazine, for fifty dollars, a large price in those days for any poetical production."

Only a fortnight before Mr. Longfellow's death the author made inquiry of him as to what pieces had been published in the Knickerbocker, and the prices paid for them. Mr. Longfellow replied good-humoredly that there were two, and that he was paid nothing. Again in the course of the evening the same matter was spoken of, and Mr. Longfellow repeated the statement, that he did not receive a dollar for either poem. One may be reasonably reluctant to spoil such a complacent story as Mr. Ward's, but Mr. Longfellow's statement ought to be decisive. The Knickerbocker paid nobody; and it was not alone among periodicals in its way of "developing native talent." Mr. N. P. Willis, in a letter addressed to the author in 1844, said, "You could not sell a piece of poetry in America."

The fact has no importance, except as showing that the authors of forty years ago wrote from an inward impulse or the desire of posthumous fame, and with the certainty that their labors could not procure them a morsel of bread. Mr. Longfellow fortunately was not dependent upon his writings for support.

In the works of most poets we see in succession the characteristic traits of youth, of maturity, and of age. We are prepared at the outset for tumults of passion, for uncalculating enthusiasm, and for an exuberance of imagery. The poetic impulse is at its height at the dawn of manhood. Years of study and experience may discipline the powers, giving material and skill both, but will never add a jot to the natural gift. The great poets have manifested their vocation before mental maturity. Shelley's "Alastor," full of natural piety, and tremulous with adolescent passion, was the fresh utterance from the heart of a boy. Nothing more absolutely of the essence of genius ever came from that unfortunate poet's pen. Pope tells us he lisped in "numbers," and his most poetical work, "The Rape of the Lock," was published at the age of 24. Byron's *prémices* were gathered at 19. Milton's "Comus" was written at 24, and the "Lycidas" at 30. Coleridge's "Lyrical Ballads" appeared when he was 26, Scott's first poems at 25, Wordsworth's at 24, Keats's "Endymion" at 24, Browning's first poems at 22, Swinburne's "Atalanta" at 21, Lamb's sonnets at 21, Hood's early poems at 26, Landor's at 21, Charles Kingsley's at 26, Felicia Hemans's at 22, Bryant's "Thanatopsis" at 19, Willis's while an undergraduate in college, Lowell's "Year's Life" at 21.

We have seen that the genius of Longfellow had also an early development; but it is noticeable that there were no evidences of immaturity in his early poems, still less of riotous passion or an overwrought diction. They have a delightful tranquillity, free from strain or effort. The lines seem to have been born in due order, and thereby the soul of the poet had its full desire, instead of being governed or turned aside by the exigencies of measure and rhyme. Thus a singular and classic completeness marked his poems from the beginning. The period of his youth glided into that of maturity imperceptibly, as the brook widens into the river.

A YOUNG PROFESSOR.

Upon his graduation in 1825, Longfellow began the study of law in his father's office; but he had no taste for the profession, and not long after was fortunate in having the opportunity to begin a literary career. The Professorship of Modern Languages was established at Bowdoin College, and the appointment was tendered to him, with leave of absence for·travel and study.

He sailed for Europe in 1826, and visited France, Spain, Italy, Germany, Holland, and England. He returned in 1829, and assumed the duties of his professorship. Mr. Peter Thacher writes as follows : —

"In the autumn of 1829, Mr. Longfellow entered upon his duties as Professor of Modern Languages in Bowdoin College. Your correspondent then saw him for the first time. He had a fine, erect figure, a complexion of great purity and delicacy, and a great deal of color. He was youthful in his appearance, and eminently handsome. His manners and conversation were charming. He possessed a most prepossessing address, and was distinguished for his courtesy and affability. His intercourse with the students was mutually satisfactory. He manifested no hauteur or stiffness. Freedom and ease predominated in the recitation-room, yet there was nothing that tended to undue familiarity. He recognized his pupils as gentlemen: they justified his estimate of them by their respectful demeanor towards their accomplished instructor. Uniformly beloved and admired by his pupils, his success as a teacher was all that could have been desired."

In the succeeding year the Freshman class numbered fifty-two, — the largest that had up to that time entered the College; and President Hamlin of Middlebury College, who entered Bowdoin that year, says that many of its members were attracted by Longfellow's reputation.

In September, 1831, he was married to Miss Mary Storer Potter, daughter of the Hon. Barrett Potter, of Portland. The Potters were early immigrants to this country, and were among the founders of the New Haven Colony.

Barrett Potter was born, March 8, 1777, at Lebanon, and was graduated at Dartmouth College in 1796. He began the practice of the law at Gorham, and was afterwards partner of Salmon Chase in Portland. He was Judge of Probate for twenty-five years, and prominent in public affairs.

Miss Potter was lovely alike in mind and in person. Her accomplishments were exceptional, especially in mathematics, as it is said she had learned to calculate eclipses. She was a proficient in languages, and her note-books and school exercises show her superior intellect and training. She made apposite citations from the poets, and indulged in occasional excursions into the domain of metaphysics. She made a most delightful impression in the society of Brunswick.

In 1833 Longfellow's first book appeared, "The Coplas of Don Jorge Manrique," with a few translations from Lope de Vega, and an

Essay on the Moral and Devotional Poetry of Spain. The poem of Manrique, a solemn and sustained effort, is deservedly admired by Spaniards, and its translation was an exceedingly difficult task. It is but just to say that Longfellow's is one of the few adequate translations, fully equalling in power and ease the original.[1]

In the same year were issued portions of "Outre-Mer," although the work was not completed until 1835.

The fame of Longfellow, both as a poet and a practical instructor, had reached Cambridge. He had prepared for his students,

[1] The following short notice of Manrique is from the pen of Professor Torricelli:—

"Jorge Manrique is a very good lyrical poet, and some of his verses on 'Love' are very pretty. He is not, however, one of the great poets of Spain. His *Coplas*, or stanzas upon the death of his father, form one of his best pieces, and, so far as I can now remember, Longfellow's translation is very good, — better, in my opinion, than the original. Such at least was the impression that it made on me when I first read it, several years ago. There was another poet of the same name, Gomez Manrique, who lived at the same time and died sev-

and used with success, grammars and other text-books of modern languages, and was recognized as a rising man. In 1835, upon the retirement of Professor George Ticknor, he was appointed to the vacant chair in Harvard College, with leave of absence as before; and with his wife again visited Europe. He spent the summer in Norway and Sweden, and the autumn and winter in Holland and Germany. His wife, whose health had been delicate for some time, died at Rotterdam, November 29, 1835. It is this lovely woman who is commemorated in the touching poem entitled "The Footsteps of Angels."

eral years later, whose poems stand higher, one especially on Human Life. He was, I think, a brother or cousin to Jorge, and the notices given in some of our cyclopædias and bibliographical dictionaries seem to confound the two and consider them as the same person. Jorge was quite young when he died, and, judging from his beginning, might have become great if his life had been spared. His being known here is due only to Longfellow. What I say is from memory, having read a great deal on the subject many years ago. Scanty as the information is, however, it is correct."

"And with them the Being Beauteous,
    Who unto my youth was given,
More than all things else to love me,
    And is now a saint in heaven.

"With a slow and noiseless footstep
    Comes that messenger divine,
Takes the vacant chair beside me,
    Lays her gentle hand in mine.

"And she sits and gazes at me,
    With those deep and tender eyes,
Like the stars, so still and saint-like,
    Looking downward from the skies.

"Uttered not, yet comprehended,
    Is the spirit's voiceless prayer,
Soft rebukes, in blessings ended,
    Breathing from her lips of air.

"O, though oft depressed and lonely,
    All my fears are laid aside,
If I but remember only
    Such as these have lived and died.'

It is by glimpses like this that we see the
tender and beautiful domestic life of the poet,
and the character of the wife of his youth.
The stanzas quoted carry an impression more
lasting than any labored eulogy.

For a year after her death he continued his studies, and in November, 1836, he returned home to enter upon his duties as " Smith Professor of Modern Languages and Literature " at Cambridge.

STUDIES ABROAD.

The years of residence in Europe were filled with thorough, earnest work. Having great natural aptitude for such studies, he mastered all the principal modern languages of Europe, and made himself familiar with the leading works in each. His subsequent labors rested largely upon this universal knowledge, as will be seen hereafter.

In 1839 he published " Hyperion," a prose romance. The hero, Paul Flemming, is an American traveller, whose few adventures form the slight thread of the story. In " Outre-Mer " and " Hyperion " may be seen maps of Longfellow's travels, and intimations of his progress in letters and art. In the first freshness of his youth he left behind him the barrenness of the New World to satiate himself with the learning, culture, tradition, and genius of Europe. Many a young man had done the same, but it was for a poet's eyes to discern the picturesque in scenes made familiar by countless books of travel, and for a poet's pen to record the larger and permanent impressions of nature and art which still charm and instruct us in the tales and sketches of " Outre-Mer," and in the wise talk of Paul Flemming. In his delicate, crystal sentences are seen, as in a camera, the towered cities, storied cathedrals, and ruined castles, as well as the mountains, lakes, and rivers, celebrated in song. But his mind is not wholly absorbed in the outward views of things; in every country he visits he divines the distinctive character, and feels the beat of the universal human heart. In "Outre-Mer" the tone changes, chapter by chapter, as the traveller crosses a national boundary. He sees what is brightest and most characteristic in each country. He looks at Spain with the eyes of Cervantes; in the old provincial cities of France, the songs of the Troubadours and the psalms of the cloisters are sounding in his ears; in Italy, he is haunted by the melodic echoes of Tasso and Petrarch; in Germany he hears the ancient bards, but still more clearly the noble strains of the new-born poets that were beginning to gladden the world. Much as his heart was drawn to the art and the joyous life of Southern Europe, his deepest feelings were awakened by the legends and soul-full poetry of the German Fatherland.

Fifty years ago English-speaking people were almost wholly ignorant of German life and literature. The general notion was of a solid, plodding, obstinate race, distinguished chiefly for beer, sausages, and military drill, — a race destitute of courtly manners and personal refinement, and without any renown except in dull and obsolete philosophy and in the arts of war. German literature was a late product, — the latest of the ages. In form and in spirit it was wholly a new development, without precedent, not indebted to classic models or to contemporaries. Germans and English alike are Goths; and the blood of a Goth is stirred by the mighty cathedrals and by the long-cherished folk-lore as it is never stirred by the lighter and more graceful forms of architecture and by the poetry that is indigenous with the descendants of the Latin race.

When English and American scholars first discovered the treasures of German poetry, there was an excitement like that which led the rush to the new continent of Columbus. We know how Carlyle was enthralled by his German masters; how Coleridge, both as poet and table-talker, exhibited himself steeped in German thought and tradition; how Hawthorne's conceptions were thought to be tinged with the mysticism of Fouqué, and the subtilty of Tieck; how Emerson got his first awakening from the same influences; and, later, how the whole Transcendental School, serenely unconscious of imitation, were talking German philosophy at second hand. Longfellow among Americans appears to have been the first to acknowledge the influence of those poets who are nearest us in blood, and whose tastes, feelings, and traditions we measurably share.

These volumes of travel are interspersed with translations from Uhland, Tieck, Müller, Salis, Goethe, and others, full of sparkle and life, and full of the deep characteristic German sentiment. At this period Longfellow had published no original poems, although the "Earlier Poems," and some of the poems in "Voices of the Night" had been written long before. Many of these, without being in any sense imitations, could not have been written by any but a German scholar, and one thoroughly in sympathy with the tender and spiritual feeling of the poets who succeeded Goethe.

The incidents of travel in "Outre-Mer"

and " Hyperion " are few. These are not guide-books, art catalogues, or itineraries. The trivial records of inns and diligences, the statistics of business and population, have no place. Instead of such details, we have only what is characteristic and enduring, set forth with a poet's instinctive art. The scenery is a charming, but unobtrusive background; while the thoughts of the wise and the immortal forms of beauty are placed in rightful prominence. In the later romance there are several brilliant sketches of men of genius. The picture of Jean Paul the Only, as a man and as a writer, is singularly felicitous and just; nearly as much must be said for the chapter on Goethe. In other chapters there are animated colloquies upon the literary life, the miseries of authors, the sanity of genius, and the proper surroundings of poets.

It may be necessary to say more plainly that what is written of " Outre-Mer " and of " Hyperion " has regard to the clear processes of the poet's development in art, rather than to any popular view of the books *as stories.* Neither book is " popular " in the ordinary sense. "Outre-Mer" is a series of gay sketches and legends, done in the easy manner of Sterne and Washington Irving One sees it is the work of a young man, an enthusiast for antiquities, fond of archaisms and old-time quaintness. " Hyperion " is more carefully constructed, more elaborate, and at times somewhat over-elaborate in style, and intended as a vehicle of poetical ideas and descriptions, rather than a fascinating romance to turn the hearts of young ladies. The careful reader will value " Hyperion" mainly for its many profound thoughts upon letters and the literary life, and for the view it gives of the poet's own deep-settled principles and objects in his chosen art.

Longfellow somewhere says, " The secret studies of an author are the sunken piers upon which is to rest the bridge of his fame, spanning the dark waters of oblivion." With this in mind we read with enlightened eyes the account he gives of the studies of his hero : —

" Paul Flemming buried himself in books, — in old dusty books. He worked his way diligently through the ancient poetic lore of Germany, from Frankish legends of St. George, and Saxon Rhyme-Chronicles, and Nibelungen-Lieds, and Helden-Buchs, and Songs of the Minnesingers and Meister-singers, and Ships of Fools, and Reynard the Foxes, and Death-Dances, and Lamentations of Damned Souls, into the bright, sunny land of harvests, where, amid the golden grain and the blue corn-flowers, walk the modern bards, and sing. . . . . His thoughts were twin-born, — the thought itself, and its figurative semblance in the outer world. Thus through the quiet still waters of his soul each image floated double, ' swan and shadow.' "

He further says : —

" In order fully to understand and feel the popular poetry of Germany one must be familiar with the German landscape. Many sweet little poems are the outbreaks of momentary feelings ; — words to which the song of birds, the rustling of leaves, and the gurgle of cool waters form the appropriate music."

Two paragraphs upon national literature show upon what broad and sure foundations, even at that early age, the mind and the art of our poet were based : —

" Nationality is a good thing to a certain extent, but universality is better. All that is best in the great poets of all countries is not what is national in them, but what is universal. Their roots are in their native soil ; but their branches wave in the unpatriotic air that speaks the same language to all men, and their leaves shine with the illimitable light that pervades all lands."

" A national literature is not the growth of a day. Centuries must contribute their dew and sunshine to it. Our own is growing slowly but surely, striking its roots downward and its branches upward, as is natural ; and I do not wish, for the sake of what some people call originality, to invert it, and try to make it grow with its roots in the air."

There is a pathetic interest in the conclusion of "Outre-Mer" : —

" As I write, the melancholy thought intrudes upon me, — To what end is all this toil?   Of what avail these midnight vigils?   Dost thou covet fame?   Vain dreamer!   A few brief days, — and what will the busy world know of thee?   Alas! this little book is but a bubble on the stream ; and although it may catch the sunshine for a moment, yet it will soon float down the swift-rushing current and be seen no more ! "

The little book might be " a bubble on the stream," but the poems that were to follow were to have a popularity and a permanency in the minds of men which have belonged to few works in any age.

THE HARVARD PROFESSOR.

In 1836 the career of our poet may be said to have fairly begun.   He came to Cambridge and took up his abode at the Craigie house, as it was then called.[1]   It was built about the year 1759 by Henry Vassall, who lies in the Cambridge church-yard under a stone bearing as an inscrip-

[1] See Drake's Historic Mansions of Middlesex.

tion only a goblet and a sun (Vas-Sol).[1] A house built by another Vassall is not far distant on the same street. The first-named house was occupied by Washington as his headquarters in the beginning of the Revolutionary war, having been purchased by the Colonial government. Afterwards it became the property of Andrew Craigie, who had been apothecary-general in the army and wealthy at one time, but who was afterwards sadly reduced in circumstances. After his death his widow let portions of the house to lodgers, and among them, at various times, besides Longfellow, were President Sparks, Edward Everett, and Joseph E. Worcester, compiler of the Dictionary. Mrs. Craigie is thus sketched by the poet Lowell, in his charming essay, "Cambridge Thirty Years Ago":—

"Here long survived him his turbaned widow, studious only of Spinoza, and refusing to molest

[1] See reference in Holmes's poem, "The Cambridge Churchyard."

the canker-worms that annually disleaved her elms, because we were all vermicular alike. She had been a famous beauty once, but the canker years had left her leafless too, and I used to wonder, as I saw her sitting always alone at her accustomed window, whether she were ever visited by the reproachful shade of him who (in spite of Rosalind) died broken-hearted for her in her radiant youth."

In 1836 Longfellow was under thirty, and an eminently handsome youth. When he raised the ponderous knocker, and summoned Mrs. Craigie, it is no wonder that she took the smooth-visaged stranger for an undergraduate or a divinity student. At his request she showed him the house, and pointed out the rooms occupied by Washington. When he said, " This is a fine room," or afterwards, " I like this also," she replied, " Ah, yes! but you can't have it." And so through the house, — " Yes, but you can't have it." She prolonged the negations until Longfellow asked the reason. " Because I don't lodge students." " But I am a professor!" That altered the case, and the poet was soon installed in the room that had been Washington's. This was the somewhat odd beginning of a residence that ended only with the poet's life.[1]

The house and its occupants will be referred to again; but it is proper to quote here two passages from "Hyperion" to show the deep yet tranquil delight which he enjoyed in looking out upon the broad landscape that stretched southward and westward from his new home. The opposite field is still open to the river, but the view on either hand has been cut off in later years by the erection of houses.

"I sit at the open window, ... and hear only the voice of the summer wind. Like black hulks, the shadows of the great trees ride at anchor on the billowy sea of grass. I cannot see the red

---

[1] During her last sickness Mrs. Craigie one day sent for Mr. Longfellow, and, remembering what her brilliant attractions had been, said, "Now that you have seen me a shrivelled old woman, you will never marry! You see what beauty comes to at last."

THE VASSALL-CRAIGIE-LONGFELLOW HOUSE IN CAMBRIDGE.

and blue flowers, but I know that they are there. Far away in the meadow gleams the silver Charles. The tramp of horses' hoofs sounds from the wooden bridge. Then all is still, save the continuous wind of the summer night. . . . . The village clock strikes; and I feel that I am not alone."

" I sit here at my pleasant chamber-window, and enjoy the balmy air of a bright summer morning, and watch the motions of the golden robin, that sits on its swinging nest on the outermost pendulous branch of yonder elm. The broad meadows and the steel-blue river remind me of the meadows of Unterseen and the river Aar; and beyond them rise magnificent snow-white clouds piled up like Alps. Thus the shades of Washington and William Tell seem to walk together on these Elysian Fields; for it was here that, in days long gone, our great patriot dwelt; and yonder clouds so much resemble the snowy Alps that they remind me irresistibly of the Swiss."

The house was much visited then and afterwards by the curious, on account of its having been the residence of Washington. Mr. Longfellow relates that, not many years ago, a plain man with country garb and solemn manners asked to be shown through the house. He went through the historic rooms with but few remarks, and those were bucolic in tone and style. The survey had been completed, and the poet stood at the open door to show the visitor out. "Much obleeged ter yer," he said, with steadfast visage; — "*and who be yer?*" "My name is Longfellow." "Longfeller?" said the man, meditatively. "Any relation to the Longfellers in Woollich, down in Maine?" "For the first time," said the poet (in telling the story), "I had a vision of the emptiness of fame."

For seventeen years (and a little more) Longfellow discharged the duties of his professorship. The place was by no means a sinecure, as he was professor and chief of the instructors besides. There were about two hundred students, and an average of half a dozen instructors (in French, Spanish, Italian, and German), and he was expected to oversee the work of all. He delivered lectures upon the modern languages and literatures, and the testimony of all his pupils is that they were admirable and helpful; they were not specimens of brilliant rhetoric merely, still less the learned dulness of a literary annalist. His quick and poetic mind seized upon parallel expressions and analogies, and enabled him to give the thoughts of foreign poets a fair and adequate English dress.

Mr. Longfellow informed the author that, though his lectures were all carefully *prepared*, they were seldom or never *written*, but were delivered freely in such words as came to mind.

He commanded the respect and won the regard of students to a remarkable degree. He was never in the least familiar, but always courteous, and retained his influence to the last. Some of the most famous of American scholars are proud to claim Longfellow as their guide into pleasant paths.

Josiah Quincy, a venerable name in our

history, was President of Harvard College at the time Mr. Longfellow began his duties, and remained in office until 1845. He was succeeded by Edward Everett, the eminent scholar and orator, who occupied the chair until 1849, when Jared Sparks, the historian, was chosen. Mr. Sparks resigned in 1853, and was succeeded by Rev. James Walker, who had been previously Professor of Moral Philosophy. The member of the Faculty with whom Mr. Longfellow was most intimate in their early years of service was Cornelius Conway Felton, Professor of Greek. Professor Felton was born in Newbury, whence the ancestors of Longfellow came. Like Longfellow, he had won his honors at an early age, having been born in the same year, 1807. He was an enthusiast in his chosen studies, and he accomplished much in many directions, as the cyclopædias and bibliographies show. He became President of the College afterwards, but his heart was always divided between his beloved Greeks and the men who were carrying forward the literary work of the day. He assisted Longfellow in the preparation of "The Poets and Poetry of Europe," and wrote many of the sketches and estimates of authors. He was a frequent contributor to the North American Review. He was one of the original dinner-party of fourteen at which the Atlantic Monthly was established. On birthday and other decorous festivities he always shone. Large in person and in brain, with an ardent temperament, perfect good-breeding, and unfailing courtesy, he was a delightful table companion. His fuller, ampler physical nature seemed to supplement the more retiring, self-restrained manner of his friend. The twin stars, whose combined radiance is brightest, are generally of diverse and complementary colors.

A fragment from Lowell's "Cambridge Thirty Years Ago" will give a glimpse of the genial Greek Professor. After quoting one of Felton's stories, Lowell adds:—

" Grecian F. (may his shadow never be less!) tells this, his great laugh expected all the while from deep vaults of chest, and then coming in at the close, hearty, contagious, mounting with the measured tread of a jovial butler who brings ancientest good-fellowship from exhaustless bins, and enough, without other sauce, to give a flavor of stalled ox to a dinner of herbs."

The exclusive pursuit of scholastic and scientific studies is often a desiccating process; and the man who can toss the moons of Saturn for their avoirdupois, or discourse on the Kritik of Kant, or annotate the Clouds of Aristophanes, is often only an intellectual machine. He may be the more perfect machine for his self-denial, but he is so much the less a well-developed man. Felton was one who toiled furiously and long, and then, when the time came, was a genial and cloud-dispelling talker, accompanying the wisdom or wit of the company with a merriment fit for Olympus on a holiday.

Another Cambridge Professor, Andrews

Norton, a friend of the great Dr. Channing, resembling him in manners and character, lived at Shady Hill, a fine estate not very far from the College grounds. He was in the Divinity School, but had always been devoted to general literature, and was one of the most accomplished men in the University. His hymns are still sung in the churches, and are among the few that have real poetic fervor as well as Christian spirit. He was a contributor to the North American Review, and was all his life engaged in useful and scholarly work. The visitor to Cambridge to-day, calling upon the son and representative of the family, Professor Charles Eliot Norton, finds a pleasant road leading him a furlong or more towards the ample old-fashioned house, standing among forest-trees upon a rounded knoll. Like Elmwood and the Vassall-Longfellow house, it is one of the places of historic interest; and the visitor carries away a lasting impression of a very quiet but beautiful home, where the library, pictures, antiques, furniture, and manners belong together, and testify to the taste and refinement of the occupants.

At this house Mr. Longfellow was a frequent visitor, especially before his second marriage in 1843, and was more intimate with the family than with any in Cambridge.

SUCCESS.

The fame of Longfellow is the growth of half a century, but his first volumes were decisive as to the place he was to hold. When the "Voices of the Night" (1839) and "Ballads" (1841) had come to the notice of the public, there was an impression as of a new planet lengthening the twilight. There was in the poems a soft radiance, serene and consoling. All classes felt it. The philosopher saw in their holy tranquillity and perfect trust the equivalent for the best outcome of his learning; and the hearts of the unlettered poor were drawn unconsciously to the divine harmonies that made them forget their sorrows. Whatever poetry had before this time dazzled the world, it may be questioned if ever in the same space there had come to the hearts of men so many sweet and tender associations, so many lessons of courage and patience, so many consolations for the stricken and afflicted. It is not solely their rare poetic beauty, their melodious flow, their perfect expression that charm us; it is their supreme and universal sway over the noblest emotions. There is not one of the "Voices of the Night" that is not familiar as household words. The lines and phrases pass current in fragments of quotation. The ideas and metrical forms are as unmistakable as doxologies or proverbs. The solemn monotone of the "Psalm of Life" was heard around the world. "The Beleaguered City," "Footsteps of Angels," "The Light of Stars," and "Flowers," have a spiritual as well as an earthly beauty. They are a gospel of good-will in music. It does not matter how often they are sung or intoned; it does not matter that the alert mind of the hearer flies before the reader along the well-known, shining track of the verse. These poems, and others in the succeeding volumes like them, are our heart treasures. We refuse criticism and comparison with the works of other poets. They are our and our children's inheritance. They are wholly without parallel in our day in the quality of touching and elevating the moral nature.

Upon these few and simple Voices and upon the few striking Ballads the fame of almost any poet might safely rest. They must appeal with undiminished force to the coming generations; just as the vicissitudes of this mortal life, — marriage, motherhood, death, — though forever repeated, yet touch each soul when its turn comes with a rapture or an agony as intense as if the experience of the hour had befallen it first in the history of creation.

And these lovely Voices and stirring Ballads in one respect exhibit the finest qualities of Longfellow's genius. They are almost the earliest of the half-century of vintages, and most racy of their native soil.

"The Wreck of the Hesperus" is deservedly admired, especially for the vigor of its descriptions. It is in truth a ballad such as former centuries knew and which are seldom written now. Its free movement, directness, and pictorial power combine to make it one of the most remarkable of the author's poems. Observe the force of this stanza: —

> "The breakers were right beneath her bows,
>   She drifted a dreary wreck,
>   And a whooping billow swept the crew
>   Like icicles from her deck."

Or this: —

> "The salt sea was frozen on her breast,
>   The salt tears in her eyes;
>   And he saw her hair like the brown sea-weed
>   On the billows fall and rise."

"The Skeleton in Armor" is perhaps the most purely imaginative of all our poet's conceptions. The various related pictures are

done with clear strokes and finished with
perfect art. It is the soul of a Viking that
chants, to the accompaniment of the shrill
north-wind and the ceaseless roar of waves.
The most consummate master of poetic art
could scarce change a line or an epithet.

There is good reason for dwelling somewhat upon the qualities of the two thin volumes of 1839 and 1841, because they had
immediate recognition as the product of a
new force in literature, and because they il-
lustrate within a small compass the qualities
of his genius and the mastery of his art. It
is far from the present writer's purpose to
attempt to conduct the reader through the
successive volumes with tedious and super-
fluous comment.

An interesting reminiscence from the pen
of the late James T. Fields [1] may be properly quoted here.

[1] It is greatly to . be lamented that Mr. Fields had not
lived to write out and publish the many anecdotes of Longfellow which had come to him during his long and intimate
acquaintance with the poet.

"The 'Psalm of Life' came into existence on a bright summer morning in July, 1838, in Cambridge, as the poet sat between two windows, at a small table, in the corner of his chamber. It was a voice from his inmost heart, and he kept it unpublished a long time; it expressed his own feelings at that time, when recovering from a deep affliction, and he hid it in his own heart for many months. The poem of 'The Reaper and the Flowers' came without effort, crystallized into his mind. 'The Light of Stars' was composed on a serene and beautiful summer evening, exactly suggestive of the poem. 'The Wreck of the Hesperus' was written the night after a violent storm had occurred, and as the poet sat smoking his pipe the Hesperus came sailing into his mind; he went to bed, but could not sleep, and rose and wrote the celebrated verses. The poem hardly caused him an effort, but flowed on without let or hindrance. On a summer afternoon in 1839, as he was riding on the beach, 'The Skeleton in Armor' rose, as out of the deep, before him, and would not be laid. One of the best known of all Longfellow's shorter poems is 'Excelsior.' That one word happened to catch his eye one autumn evening in 1841, on a torn piece of newspaper, and straightway his imagination took fire at it. Taking up a piece of paper, which happened to be the back of a letter received that day from Charles Sumner, he crowded it with verses. As first written down, ' Excelsior ' differs from the perfected and published version, but it shows a rush and glow worthy of its author." [1]

Two years later came " The Spanish Student," a play for the closet rather than the stage, with a well conceived, if not wholly original plot, natural and living characters, and containing lines and passages of unmistakable poetical merit. This appears to have been almost the only diversion our poet ever allowed himself, unless we except certain scenes in " The Wayside Inn," and the frolics of the monks in " The Golden Legend." Longfellow's was a bright, cheery, and lovable nature, but he was never a leader in mirth. His ready smile and quick glance of intelligence showed how he felt the point of wit; but he was generally a pleased

---

[1] Boston Daily Globe, March 25, 1882.

spectator rather than an actor in such encounters.

"The Spanish Student" is saturated with the national qualities, and its perfect keeping shows how thoroughly the poet had studied the popular traits, which remain so quaint, picturesque, and enduring. It is a gay and often brilliant picture of the manners of a remarkable people. It is a fair complement to the high solemnity of Manrique's poem, and is likely to be long enjoyed; but it has not the invention, the blazing wit, or the unexpected turns that mark comedies of the highest rank.

ANTISLAVERY POEMS.

The "Poems on Slavery," published in the same year, show Longfellow in another light. In 1843 the public sentiment of the United States, guided by politicians, cottonspinners, and bankers, was almost wholly in favor of a great national wrong. To keep humanitarian ideas out of politics, to continue manufactures with profit, and to bind the people together in successful business, leaving morals out, was the aim of legislators and leaders. The voices of Channing, Garrison, Jay, and Sumner were unheard or scorned. The warnings and weighty counsels of Jefferson had been forgotten. The Union was a pyramid whose lower strata were crushed human hearts. The pulpit and the press were silent, if not openly favorable to the continuance of the nation's shame and curse.

Longfellow published his poems, full of indignant feeling, yet tempered by Christian charity, and so gave the great influence of his name to the despised cause. "The Slave singing at Midnight" and "The Quadroon Girl" produced a strong impression. But the stanza most frequently quoted was the last one of "The Warning." Read now in the light of later events, it sounds strangely prophetic : —

"There is a poor, blind Samson in this land,
  Shorn of his strength and bound in bonds of steel,
Who may, in some grim revel, raise his hand,
  And shake the pillars of this Commonweal,
Till the vast Temple of our liberties
A shapeless mass of wreck and rubbish lies."

A man of Longfellow's quiet, scholarly habits and refined taste could not have been an agitator. The bold denunciation of a Boanerges would ill have befitted his lips. He would have felt out of place upon the platform of an antislavery meeting. But his influence, though quiet, was pervasive, and it was a comfort to many earnest men to know that the first scholars and poets were in sympathy with their hopes, their prayers and labors.

Among the most eminent of the Abolitionists was Ralph Waldo Emerson, and the friendship between him and our poet begun at an early date. Certain critics who would like to disparage Longfellow have been in the habit of applying to his verses an Emersonian or transcendental test, as if there were a natural antagonism between Cambridge and Concord. But this is a mode of warfare that belongs to the subalterns: between our poet and the great philosopher there have always existed the warmest personal relations and the most solid regard. Between men truly great, however diverse in genius, the narrowness that insists upon likeness has no place. Upon abstruse and especially moral topics Mr. Emerson was a natural leader. He did not argue up to propositions. He calmly announced them, like a seer or prophet. Though Garrison was the moving spirit of the antislavery party, Emerson was the Nestor, the intellectual head of it.

Longfellow had been intimate also with Dr. Channing, as his poetical tribute shows.

Another devoted friend, destined afterwards to advance the standard of freedom, was Charles Sumner. While still a very young man, hardly one-and-twenty, he had proposed to himself a career, and had bent all the powers of his active and powerful mind to prepare himself for it. The preparation of a " statesman " in later days is sometimes of a different nature. Mr. Sumner was ignorant of all the arts of politics. He merely studied law, treaties, history, and ethics, that he might fit himself to be a legislator. His reading covered a wide field, and the knowledge he had was always at command. Perhaps his learning was sometimes oppressive to himself, like the Roman soldier's outfit, which got the name of *impedimenta.* Those who took their learning at second hand — quoting from quoters — considered him pedantic; and it must be said that the time for formal orations was going by, and the time for actual debate had not come. It is not likely that Demosthenes could turn a vote to-day in the House of Commons; and Cicero would be badgered into confusion in the first ten minutes of an exordium before our Congress. Somewhat too stately and too full of quotation as Mr. Sumner's speeches are, they are full of vital thought and energy, and in their completeness cover the whole field of argument. They and their author belong to history. It was over forty years ago that Mr. Sumner became an acquaintance, and then a friend; and he was for a long time in the habit of dining with Longfellow every Sunday. The writer remembers frequently seeing Sumner's tall figure, in a cloak, striding over Cambridge Bridge, or riding part of the way, with knees drawn up, in the long, old-fashioned coaches. His face, which was naturally stern, had a pleasant smile as he spoke of the anticipated pleasure. Like the bottles in the poet's gay verses to Agassiz, Mr. Sumner's smiles seemed to say, " I am to dine with Longfellow." In Longfellow's study Sumner's youthful portrait in crayon, by Eastman Johnson, hangs with the portraits of Felton, Hawthorne, and Emerson, done by the same artist. How young they all look! Charming faces, with no prefiguring of destiny in their calm eyes.

The attachment was mutual and sincere, and readers may see the expression of it in the poem "Three Friends of Mine."

These friendships are merely touched upon at this point to show Longfellow's clear relation to the antislavery cause and to some of its ablest and most scholarly representatives.

It is proper to add, that many of Longfellow's poems had a profound purpose and significance not always suspected by readers. "The Arsenal at Springfield" is one of his most splendid productions, and by most it is admired as a poem only. But it becomes historic when we remember that Sumner had lately delivered the great oration in Boston on "The True Grandeur of Nations," (July 4, 1845,) in which he inveighed against the wickedness of war as a means of settling national disputes; and that soon after came this noble, almost inspired poem, with its vivid picture of war's desolations and its holy prophecy of peace.

"Down the dark future, through long generations,
  The echoing sounds grow fainter and then cease ;
And like a bell, with solemn, sweet vibrations,
  I hear once more the voice of Christ say, ' Peace !'

"Peace ! and no longer from its brazen portals
  The blast of War's great organ shakes the skies!
But beautiful as songs of the immortals,
  The holy melodies of love arise."

HIS SECOND MARRIAGE.

"Hyperion," in some respects, gives the history of the poet's inner life. Paul Flemming begins his tour under the shadow of a great sorrow. The wife of his youth, the "Being Beauteous," with her infant, lay in the churchyard, and the husband and father felt the bereavement with an intensity of grief which only such delicate natures can know. But after a time there was a change. Grief had chastened the poet, but had not left him in despair. He was still young, and before him might be supposed to lie a long road to be traversed, — with new duties to be done, new achievements, new hopes, and the exceeding great reward of faithful love. In this mood he met a lady who in the story is called Mary Ashburton, and, becoming interested at first, is in the end passionately devoted to her. She is drawn with admirable lines, and becomes a real person to the reader. Her beauty, her accomplishments, her family pride, all naturally become her, as an Englishwoman; and in her impenetrable reserve we see a disastrous ending for the poet's earnest suit.

The original of this brilliant portrait was Miss Frances Elizabeth Appleton, daughter of Nathan Appleton, a distinguished citizen of Boston. Her surviving brother is Mr. Thomas Gold Appleton, a well-known author and a connoisseur in art. She was indeed possessed of every grace of mind and person that could charm the soul of a poet. Her remarkable beauty was fitly accompanied by a serene dignity of manner; and it may be added that, later, as a matron, she was even more beautiful than in her fresh youth. With her children about her she looked a proud Cornelia. Among the many memorable persons who during the generations dwelt in the Vassall house, the name and lovely presence of this admirable woman come first to mind.

The precise time at which Mr. Longfellow met Miss Appleton is not important. The romance was published in 1839, and it embraces necessarily an antecedent experience. The rejection of Paul Flemming's suit was possibly true; but it is known that, whatever final decision Mary Ashburton in the story may have come to, Miss Appleton cherished a deep regard for her suitor, and the intimacy gradually ripened into love. Their marriage took place in 1843, when our poet was in his thirty-sixth year. He purchased the Vassall-Craigie house, and from that time forward it was his home.

Five children were the offspring of this marriage, — two sons, and three daughters.

Ernest W. Longfellow, the eldest, is an eminent artist. Charles Appleton Longfellow served for two years as a captain of cavalry in our late civil war. Edith, the second daughter, is married to Richard H. Dana, third of the name, grandson of the poet and son of the eminent lawyer and publicist who wrote "Two Years Before the Mast." The other daughters, Alice and Anna, remain at home, and are unmarried. The three daughters were painted in a group by the late T. Buchanan Read, artist and poet both, and the picture is well known to the public by engravings and photographs.

Of the exceeding beauty of the Longfellow home much has been written. The reader remembers the poet's reference to the former majestic occupant: —

> "Once, ah, once, within these walls,
> One whom memory oft recalls,
> The Father of his Country, dwelt.
> And yonder meadows broad and damp
> The fires of the besieging camp
> Encircled with a burning belt.

> Up and down these echoing stairs,
> Heavy with the weight of cares,
> Sounded his majestic tread ;
> Yes, within this very room
> Sat he in those hours of gloom,
> Weary both in heart and head."

The grounds are large and set with fine trees, with open vistas intervening. The children had a fresh country air and space for rambles. The house is at a suitable distance from the street, and there is an atmosphere of quiet seldom seen so near a great city. The poet had his rooms and his hours, and while the family could enjoy their perfect freedom, the size of the house and the admirable domestic arrangements left the master leisure and liberty to pursue his manifold studies and to fashion his poetical creations.

In this as in many other respects Longfellow was exceedingly fortunate. Poverty, narrow accommodations, noise and illness, are enough at times to disenchant even a genius; and many an aspiration has been stifled,

VIEW OF THE LONGFELLOW HOUSE FROM THE LAWN, ON THE NORTH SIDE.

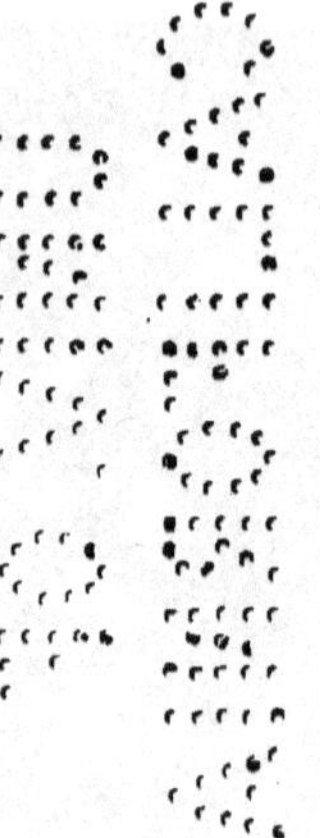

many a work of art injured in its progress, by the annoying surroundings in which it was wrought. So far as human power can judge, Longfellow was in the best possible situation for the development of his powers. He had had the best training which was possible at the time, and he had used every opportunity; he had never known the distress of poverty or sickness; he had been able to accumulate rare books, and to feast upon the art of Europe.

It has been previously mentioned that Charles Sumner was a very intimate friend of Longfellow, and it may be pleasant to see the references in his letters to the happy marriage. Writing to John Jay, at New York, May 25, 1843, Mr. Sumner says : —

" You will probably find Longfellow a married man, for he is now engaged to Miss Fannie Appleton, the Mary Ashburton of ' Hyperion,' a lady of the greatest sweetness, imagination, and elevation of character, with striking personal charms."

August 13, 1843, he writes from Boston to George W. Greene : —

" You will find dear Longfellow married to the beautiful and most lovely Mary Ashburton. They were married on July 13. They will rejoice to see you. They will linger among her friends in Berkshire until Saturday, August 19, when they will return to Cambridge, and she will commence her life as *Professorinn*."

To Professor Mittermaier of Heidelberg, Germany, Mr. Sumner wrote : —

" You have heard of the happiness of Longfellow, who is married to a most beautiful lady, possessing every attraction of character and intelligence."

To Dr. Francis Lieber, Jan. 6, 1843 : —

" You complain that L.'s friends will spoil him by praise. You little know the sternness with which his friends judge his works before they are published."

To the same, July 13, 1843 : —

" I do not think it essential that the first poets of an age should write *war* odes. Our friend has a higher calling, and it is Longfellow's chief virtue to have apprehended it. His poetry does not rally to battle, but it affords succor and strength to bear the ills of life. There are six or seven pieces of his far superior, as it seems to me, to anything I know of Uhland or Körner, — calculated to do more good, — to touch the soul to finer issues; pieces that will live to be worn near the hearts of men when the thrilling war-notes of Campbell and Körner will be forgotten. . . . . I would rather be the author of ' A Psalm of Life,' ' The Light of Stars,' ' The Reaper,' and ' Excelsior,' than of those rich pieces of Gray. I think Longfellow without a rival near his throne in America. I might go further: I doubt if there is any poet now alive, and not older than he, who has written so much and so well. . . . . Longfellow is to be happy for a fortnight in the shades of Cambridge, then to visit his wife's friends in Berkshire, then his own in Portland."

POETS AND POETRY OF EUROPE.

For nearly two years Mr. Longfellow devoted himself to the work of presenting to English readers a view of the poetry of contemporary nations. As was intimated before, he was assisted by his friend, Professor Felton. This collection includes nearly four hundred pieces, translated from ten different languages. Mr. Longfellow wrote the introductions, and made many of the translations. Some of the latter are acknowledged, but many of them are anonymous. Mr. Longfellow said to the writer, that among many narrow-minded persons the notion of a translation was that of job-work, requiring no original power; and as he had published a considerable number in former volumes, he thought it not best to put his name to all the versions he had made. He thought that a certain kind of depreciation followed a translator, and he did not care to give any more occasion for ill-natured remark than was necessary. It is to be hoped that memoranda exist by which the extent of our obligations to him may be known hereafter.

Grammarians tell us that nice points in the

structure of sentences are never apprehended by a student in any one language; it is only when two reflections of the same thought are shown, as in a duplex mirror, that there is a perfect appreciation of a stereoscopic effect. Similarly it is so in poetry. To give an actual equivalent of a great poem in another language, with its weight of thought, its allusions, images, rhythm, and its after-suggestiveness, requires a poet hardly, if at all, inferior to the original maker.

It was far from "job-work" to make the noble volume referred to. Doubtless the work had been in mind for many years, and the pilgrim of Outre-Mer and the hero of Hyperion had been silently accumulating the wealth of materials.

THE BELFRY OF BRUGES.

A year later (1846) appeared two thin volumes of selected poetry, entitled "The Waif" and "The Estray," now very scarce and much sought by collectors. The proem to the first,

"The Day is Done," &c., is perhaps as widely popular as any production of our poet; and, with the exception of the comparison in the last lines of the first stanza, it is one of great merit. It is a charming poem, soothing in tone, full of noble images, and not above the comprehension of average readers. Musical people cannot but regret that it has been so long associated with the vapid and commonplace melody written for it by Balfe. Probably no stanza has been so universally quoted as the concluding one of this poem:—

> "And the night shall be filled with music,
> And the cares that infest the day
> Shall fold their tents, like the Arabs,
> And as silently steal away."

In the same year was published "The Belfry of Bruges, and Other Poems," a volume whose general tone corresponds with the "Voices of the Night" and the "Ballads," and which had the effect of widening the circle of the poet's fame. Whatever may come afterwards, the reader may surely pause here to dwell upon these poems, confident that nothing more characteristic, more full of delightful associations, is to come. The poet has grown stronger, and paints with more decisive lines. The pictures of Bruges, and of Nuremberg, the mediæval museum and memorial of Albert Dürer, are full of life and color.

But the gem of the volume is "The Arsenal at Springfield," a poetical complement to Sumner's "True Grandeur of Nations," a series of magnificent images wrought with surpassing art. It is a poem of high rank, if not the highest, and any great English poet, living or dead, might have been proud to acknowledge it.

"The Old Clock on the Stairs," in the same volume, is one of the fortunate poems which have become a part of the domestic life and love of a generation. The "old-fashioned country seat" in which the clock stood was the house of the poet's father-in-law, at Pittsfield, Mass.; and the beautiful

clock, which is now in the possession of Mr.
T. G. Appleton, of Boston, continues serenely
ticking,

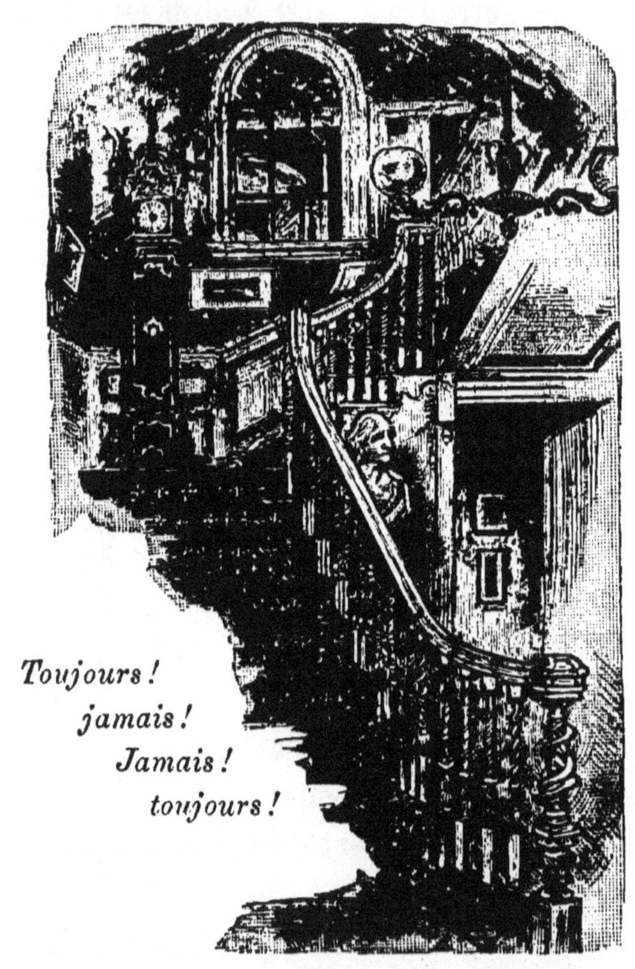

CRITICISM.

But it is time to consider some of the trials as well as the pleasures of the poet's life. If the friends of Longfellow were inclined to spoil him with praise, there was a sharp corrective ready to be administered by Poe.

Although there is at present a feeling of friendship between the literati of New York and New England, there was a time, some thirty or forty years ago, when there was no affection wasted. The beginning or new birth of literature in America was nearly contemporaneous in New York and Boston; although the earliest of our successful modern authors was a New-Yorker. Before the days of railroads there was far less intercourse than now, and the two cities were for all purposes as far apart as Paris and Berlin.

Longfellow, whose travels had been almost always in Europe, visited New York seldom. The reader remembers, doubtless, a very large and singularly bad engraving, formerly very commonly seen, entitled " Washington Irving and his Friends." Among Massachusetts authors were represented Prescott, with an inane expression, Holmes, a wretched burlesque, and Longfellow, with a pleasant, dandyish air and hyacinthine locks. These, with Bancroft, Emerson, and others, were grouped about the central figure, Irving, who was made to look like a successful tallow-chandler. It was a picture to put one in a rage for destruction. Now in truth Longfellow met Irving in Spain in 1827, while the latter was there writing his Columbus, and never saw him afterwards. There was always a pleasant feeling, but no intimacy. They did not happen to come together. So with regard to Bryant; Longfellow met him about the year 1830, *once.* Afterwards, in 1836, the two poets met and had a friendly conversation at Heidelberg. They never met again.

It may be inferred that the lesser writers of New York had seen Longfellow still less.

So when Poe in "The Broadway Journal" (also in Graham's Magazine) opened his batteries upon our poet, it appeared much like a shot from a foreign camp. But it may be added, that scarcely any eminent writer of the last generation escaped an attack from him. He cherished for Boston, New England, and the North, a pure and quenchless flame of hatred. He had certain theories of art which he assumed to be axiomatic. He measured modern poems by the classic mete-wands, oblivious of the fact that English syllables have no radical character of long and short, and that any exact reproduction of the classic metres is impossible. He declared that a poem which could not be read at a sitting was no poem,—a decision that rules out nearly every production which the world agrees to call great. His sense of melody in verse was, no doubt, exquisite, and he pleased himself so much with the satin surfaces of things that the meaning beneath was of less moment. If he illustrated metres or assonances, his own verses were often the chosen examples. One can see that he petted his own creations, and loved to turn them in various lights to display their sheen. As an instance of the possibilities of language he used to quote in his critical papers,

"And the silken sad uncertain rustling of each purple curtain,"

— a line for a sentimental milliner.

To show his temper and his sense of justice a few paragraphs are quoted. When Hawthorne's "Twice Told Tales" was published, — a volume that no other living man could have written, — Poe said : "The fact is, that, if Mr. Hawthorne were really original, he could not fail of making himself felt by the public. But the fact is he is *not* original in any sense." Poe admits that there is a sense of newness in Hawthorne, but says it comes from an imitation of Tieck. He quotes a passage from "Howe's Masquerade," and attempts to show that it was copied from his own "William Wilson." His advice to Hawthorne at the conclusion of his review is characteristic: "Let him mend his pen, get a bottle of visible ink, cut Mr. Alcott, hang (if possible) the editor of 'The Dial,' and throw out of the window to the pigs all his odd numbers of the North American Review." He recommends a new motto for the North American, altered from Sterne: "As we rode along the valley, we saw a herd of asses on the top of one of the mountains, — how they viewed and *reviewed* us." He elsewhere mentions "the cultivated old clergymen of the North American Review"; — "that ineffable buzzard, the North American Review"; and "the Fabian family, who live (upon beans) about Boston." He has only a sneer for Emerson, as an imitator of Carlyle.

His warmest words are for Amelia B. Welby, a writer of a school that has passed away. Mrs. Welby's verse was melodious, full of bright adjectives and epithets, sweet, sensuous, and melancholy by turns, and about as real as muslin flowers or a stage cascade. It was enough for Poe that her poems were according to the canons he had laid down. In his own poems (it may be added) the superficial glamour and the tricks of syllabification were the fleeting charm. In "The Raven" there is no substratum of *feeling*. A man who is really haunted by remorse would not remark "the silken sad uncertain rustling" of anything; nor would there be any suggestion to such a soul in the iterated refrain,

"Quoth the raven, Nevermore."

This is not remorse, still less repentance. There is not a line in the poem that might not have been written by Mephistopheles while waiting for Faust and Margaret in the garden. It was the fashion forty years ago to play sentiment, and nearly all the "poets" of America were doing it, from Poe and Mrs. Welby downward.

The weight of Poe's wrath fell upon Longfellow. For an Ishmael, such as he was, it was enough that Longfellow was beloved in

Boston, and that he was becoming the most popular poet in the language. If he had been the sole assailant, the attack would have been less formidable. But the views of the extreme transcendental school were almost as hostile as Poe's, although for different reasons. The transcendentalists thought they had risen above the concrete into the domain of the abstract, not to say the absolute. Poetry that dealt with the aspects of nature, or with any outward affairs, was for them an A B C book. For them poetry must consist of sonorous enigmas, Orphic sayings, sententious nothings.

But every true poet rests on the natural world *first.* He may aspire, or soar at times, but he cannot take upon himself the character and functions of a bodiless intelligence. Somewhere *between* heaven and earth is the poet's sphere. While mortality endures, its natural incidents must affect all men, and the poet most of all. But some of the transcendentalists were impatient with all those who did not bestride broomsticks and sail away moonwards. Longfellow, though esteemed by them as a man, was not their poet. Their feeling against him was not expressed in print, but of its existence there is no doubt. The writer well remembers the current talk among disciples of this school in Boston, in 1852, and afterwards. It is therefore not astonishing to read in one of Poe's diatribes the statement that Margaret Fuller called Longfellow "a booby," and Lowell "a wretched poetaster." Mr. F. B. Sanborn mentions that she called Longfellow "a dandy Pindar."

We will give a few specifications from Poe's indictment of Longfellow as a plagiarist.

He collates at length the "Midnight Mass for the Dying Year" with Tennyson's "The Death of the Old Year." But the reader sees that the verbal resemblances are slight, and every one knows that the personification of the Old Year as a dying man is as old as mankind.

He quotes a scene from " The Spanish Student," and then one from his own drama, " Politian," alleging that Longfellow had copied from him. The only feature in common is that in each scene there is a lady with a servant, and that the lady's reading is interrupted by occasional comment. There is not the least resemblance between the passages, either in thought or diction.

He avers that Longfellow stole from Bryant's " Thanatopsis " the closing lines of his " Autumn "; that he took from Sir Philip Sidney the saying, " Look into thy heart and write "; that the image of the heart's " beating funeral marches to the grave " is from Henry King, Bishop of Chichester.

Poe's review of " The Spanish Student " contains a number of excerpts which are of themselves sufficient evidence of Longfellow's poetical power and skill. He thereupon proceeds to tear the plot as flimsy, and to depreciate the general tone as borrowed from Cervantes, and he "regrets" that Long-fellow wrote it.

In the review of the "Ballads," he says that Longfellow's skill is great and his ideality high, but that his conception of the aims of poesy is *all wrong.* Poetry, according to Poe, is "the creation of novel moods of beauty in form, in color, in sound, and in sentiment." "If a thought can be expressed in prose it is no theme for poetry." We can commend these statements without qualification, and at the same time claim that "The Village Blacksmith," "The Wreck of the Hesperus," and "The Skeleton in Armor," are eminent examples of "novel forms of beauty" in all respects.

He objects to the translations, — especially to those in hexameter measure, concerning which something is said elsewhere.

In the "Marginalia" Poe states the case of a detected pickpocket, and then says, "It is impossible, we should think, to imagine a more sickening spectacle than that of the plagiarist who walks among mankind with an erecter step, and who feels his heart beat with a prouder impulse, on account of plaudits which he is conscious are the due of another."

Elsewhere he says that Longfellow is "the most audacious imitator in America." But he makes "no charge of moral delinquency"; surely not, after the parallel with the pickpocket! With a sudden gleam of good sense, he declares that "All literary history demonstrates that for the most frequent and palpable plagiarisms we must search the works of the most eminent poets."

Emerson says that great geniuses are the most indebted men. Burton in his "Anatomy of Melancholy" speaks of writers "who compound books as apothecaries compound medicines, pouring out of old bottles into new ones." The wisdom of mankind lies in scattered sayings of far away or unknown origin. "Art is long and time is fleeting" is from the Greek. Such fragments are

the property of any man who aptly uses
them.

> " Though old the thought and oft exprest,
>   'T is his at last who says it best."

Milton's obligations to Dante, to Fletcher, and
others, are well known. The idea of the line,

> " And aery tongues that syllable men's names,"

is from Marco Polo's travels. He was a royal
borrower, but the gold he took was stamped
with his own image, and made his own forever. Shakespeare laid the whole world
under contribution, but what characteristic
line of his own could be imitated? Scott's
most beautiful imagery came from the old
ballads he had been nourished upon. The
pretty couplet,

> " E'en the light harebell raised its head
>   Elastic from her airy tread,"

is from an old poet. Some of the finest
touches in Tennyson are from Theocritus.
Lowell's happy simile,

> " All ways to once her feelins flew,
>   Like sparks in burnt-up paper,"

came (unconsciously, perhaps) from a play-
ful sentence in a letter from Banister to Dean
Swift. But to multiply instances would be
attempting to give the history and pedigree
of poetical ideas and images.[1]

In Longfellow's youth the treasures of
German literature might be said to have
been just discovered. The treasures themselves, though rich and unique, are not old.
Longfellow collected the poetry of Europe,
translating parts of it himself; and it is natural that his memory should have been stored
with the thoughts of congenial minds. The
talk of "receptivity" is nonsense. Every
man is receptive in proportion to his reading
and knowledge. Excepting Goethe, and perhaps Schiller, there was none of them more
original and suggestive than himself; and if
he borrowed, he communicated as well. It
has been mentioned that he had been a stu-

---

[1] For a large and curious collection of poetical imitations
and resemblances, see Disraeli's Curiosities of Literature, VoL
II. p. 260.

dent of scenery and of historic incidents in his foreign travels; and his own reminiscences, together with the memories of the foreign poems which he had given to the world, must have formed a wonderful store of thought and incident for his own use. Is not the world richer thereby? Is not the poet himself more affluent, more full of resource, possessed of more varied power? In certain authors the individuality is so strong that it is a limitation. Many a popular poet has drawn all his inspiration and devoted all his powers to the little spot that gave him birth. Such poems may be full of genius, and yet after a time pall by reason of sameness. Who could endure a concert in which every piece was written and performed in one key? Laying aside other data of comparison, it must be admitted that there is not to be found in the works of any other poet such a variety, both as regards themes and treatment, as in the cycle of Longfellow's poems. Of one we may say he is intensely English, or that he is Scotch to the marrow; of another, that he has the soul of a Puritan, or the imagination of a German, or the gayety and wit of a Frenchman; but it is only of Longfellow we can say that his genius disregards geographical boundaries, is bound to the traditions of no one race, and with universal sympathy has dissolved and assimilated the poetry of our time. He alone is entitled to be called the poet of humanity.

Time has settled this controversy. " The Raven " and the few other poems of that brilliant and erratic genius will be remembered, but his shallow and spiteful criticism of Longfellow and Hawthorne will be read only by the curious in literary history. It has been often said that Poe was as great a critic as poet, and there are passages in his works which show great acumen and originality of view. But justice is the basis of criticism, or should be; and a man of Poe's temper and principles could never be just.

He might deal fairly and tenderly by poets over whose graves the daisies were growing; but he could not control his jealousy and his sectional feeling with regard to prosperous authors still living as rivals in public favor.

William Winter, whose youth was passed in Cambridge, has given a characteristic picture of the placid manner of Longfellow, when conversing upon the same topic. Mr. Winter says:—

" For the infirmities of humanity he was charity itself, and he shrank from harshness as from a positive sin. 'It is the prerogative of the poet,' he once said to me, in those old days, 'to give pleasure; but it is the critic's province to give pain.' He had, indeed, but a slender esteem for the critic's province. Yet his tolerant nature found excuses for even as virulent and hostile a critic as his assailant and traducer, Edgar Allan Poe,—of whom I have heard him speak with genuine pity. His words were few and unobtrusive, and they clearly indicated his consciousness that Poe had grossly abused and maligned him; but instead of resentment for injury, they displayed only sorrow for an unfortunate and half-crazed adversary. There was a little volume of Poe's poems — an English edition — on the library table, and at sight of this I was prompted to ask Longfellow if Poe had ever personally met him, — 'because,' I said, ' if he had known you, it is impossible he could have written about you in such a manner.' He answered that he had never seen Poe, and that the bitterness was doubtless due to a deplorable literary jealousy. Then, after a pause of musing, he added, very gravely, ' My works seemed to give him much trouble, first and last; but Mr. Poe is dead and buried, and I am alive and still writing, — and that is the end of the matter. I never condescended to answer Mr. Poe's attacks; and I would advise you now, at the outset of your literary career, never to take notice of any attacks that may be made upon you. Let them all pass.' He then took up the volume of Poe, and, turning the leaves, particularly commended the stanzas entitled ' For Annie,' and ' The Haunted Palace.' Then, still speaking of criticism, he mentioned the great number of newspaper and magazine articles about his own writings that were received by him, — sent apparently by their writers. ' I look at the first few lines,' he said, ' and if I find that the article has been written in a pleasant spirit, I read it through ; but if I find that the intention is to wound, I drop the paper into my fire, and so dismiss it. In that way one escapes much annoyance.' " [1]

. It is often assumed that the general judgment of the world may be relied upon as sound. And this is true, if one allows time enough for that judgment to work itself clear. It took a century to establish the rank of Milton, so great and so persistent was the prejudice against him as a Puritan and as Cromwell's Secretary of State. And it frequently happens, upon the appearance of a man of genius whose work is absolutely new, that one man alone sees the new light. This was the case with regard to Hawthorne. Longfellow was not only attached to our great romancer as a friend and college classmate : he saw the unfolding of a wonderfully poetic, sensitive nature, and the development of a power in dissecting souls such as few men since Shakespeare have shown.

[1] New York Tribune, March 30, 1882.

When Hawthorne's "Twice Told Tales" was published (1837) Longfellow wrote of it thus : —

"It comes from the hand of a man of genius. Everything about it has the freshness of morning and of May. These flowers and green leaves of poetry have not the dust of the highway upon them. They have been gathered fresh from the secret places of a peaceful and gentle heart. There flow deep waters, silent, calm, and cool; and the green trees look into them, and God's blue heaven."

"This book, though in prose, is written nevertheless by a poet."

" Another characteristic is the exceeding beauty of his style. It is as clear as running waters. Indeed, he uses words as mere stepping-stones upon which with a free and youthful bound his spirit crosses and recrosses the bright and rushing stream of thought." [1]

Boston then as now had its editors and critics, but who of them saw the beauty

[1] See the notice in "Driftwood," a collection of early essays.

which Longfellow so eloquently praised? Not five hundred copies of the book were sold; and indeed the genius of Hawthorne was wholly in obscurity until the publication of "The Scarlet Letter." Fame was sure to come, for such a book could not be hidden; but its sudden popularity came from a very singular and extraneous circumstance. In the "Introductory," Hawthorne had sketched with powerful lines some of the best known citizens of Salem. It was admirably done, if one could forget its apparent cruelty. Hawthorne was smarting under the loss of his office, which occurred when the Whigs came into power; and in the freshness of his disappointment he laid about him with vigorous blows. The "Introductory" got into politics, and was attacked and defended, and so the book had a widespread and gratuitous advertisement.

Suppose Hawthorne had died before writing "The Scarlet Letter"! Where would have been his fame? Where was the justice of the general judgment? Unpalatable as the fact may be, there are few men living at any time who are masters of a pure and lucid style of writing, and almost as few who recognize it. For the bulk of mankind the turgidity of certain historians, or the slip-shod English of the citizen who writes in the newspapers on some emergency, is just as satisfactory as the exquisite grace of Curtis, or the limpid beauty of Hawthorne.

EVANGELINE.

If a plebiscite could be taken among women in the English-speaking world, it is probable that "Evangeline," published in 1847, would be designated as the most attractive of Longfellow's longer poems. The general account of its origin is, that Hawthorne had heard the story upon which the poem is based, and at first thought of making it the subject of a romance, but, finding it unsuited to his purpose, gave it to Longfellow. The story is thus set down in Hawthorne's Note Book: —

" H. L. C—— heard from a French Canadian a story of a young couple in Acadie. On their marriage day all the men in the Province were summoned to assemble in the church to hear a proclamation. When assembled, they were all seized and shipped off, to be distributed through New England, among them the new bridegroom. His bride set off in search of him, wandered about New England all her lifetime, and at last, when she was old, she found her bridegroom on his death-bed. The shock was so great that it killed her likewise."

Mr. Longfellow, not long before his death, related to the writer the story as he remembered it. Hawthorne came one day to dine with the poet, and brought with him Mr. H. L. Connolly. At the table Mr. Connolly told the Acadian story, just as Hawthorne has noted it down, and some conversation followed upon its suitableness for a romance or poem. Hawthorne declared that he was not drawn to it, and did not believe he could make anything of it. Longfellow, on the other hand, was greatly impressed by it, and saw in it the germ of a pathetic idyl. Hawthorne then said that he would waive any claim, and that Longfellow was welcome to it.[1]

The scenery in the poem is generally admired, but it may be surprising to know that Mr. Longfellow was never in the Acadian valley. Its beauty has been often described, and the poet, who know so well similar landscapes in Maine, had no difficulty in painting an ideal background for his charming story.

After reproving Poe,

"Who talks like a book of iambs and pentameters
In a way to make people of common sense damn metres,"

it would be an abuse of the reader's patience to enter upon any critical discussion of the hexameter measure. The way to enjoy the poem is to read it in time with a musical inner sense, but without any exaggerated

---

[1] Mr. Longfellow thought (March, 1882) that Connolly was still living.

stress of voice. The cæsural pause one naturally divines. It does not help in the least to think of the

"Arma virumque cano ‖ Trojæ qui primus ab oris,"

for accent is the sole basis of English verse. There is no " quantity." The obvious difficulty is in the want of spondees in the language. Whoever wishes to give examples finds it necessary to use compound words, and they are not many nor always poetical in suggestion. English words of two syllables are generally accented forcibly upon the one or the other, and seldom are evenly pronounced. " Firm-set," " deep-voiced," " long-drawn," — such are the combinations which the poet must use. And as for dactyls, the ear is guided solely by accent. If the line trips along, we must call it dactylic, though the stockades of consonants would have shocked an artist in Greek or Latin hexameter. And the lines in Evangeline do move with varying beauty ; they are usually less spondaic than the classic models, but they have an elastic, long-swinging movement, and well-placed cæsura. Some lines are strongly spondaic; as where the poet, with a nice sense of the firm basis required, mentions the trees, how they

"Stand like | harpers | hoar || with | beards that | rest on
   their | bosoms."

The hexameter measure has seldom been successfully employed in English, or in any modern language: with the exception of Goethe's "Hermann und Dorothea," "Evangeline" is the one conspicuous example.[1] And the art of Longfellow is exquisite in suiting the measure to the sentiment of the lines, and by fixing the cæsura so as to de-

---

[1] "The Bothie" of Arthur Hugh Clough is said by scholars to be more like Greek in metrical correctness.

Coleridge has translated two fine lines from Schiller, in which the measure is exemplified: —

"Strongly it bears us along in swelling and limitless billows,
   Nothing before and nothing behind but the sky and the ocean."

"Schwindelnd trägt er dich fort auf rastlos strömenden Wogen
   Hinter dir siehst du, du siehst vor dir nur Himmel und Meer."

fend against monotony. There is nothing of the distressing *see-saw* or *canter* in "Evangeline." Every line is musical in its own way, and by contrast the beauty of every passage is heightened and sustained.

The poem besides its perfect movement has the indefinable charm of perfect keeping. The tone is always dictated by the poet's perfect sense of fitness. Lowell says : —

" Had Theocritus written in English, not Greek,
  I believe that his exquisite sense would scarce change a line
  In that rare, tender, virgin-like pastoral, Evangeline."

All the world knows the pathetic story, and most persons, it may be supposed, have read it in haste, to follow the sad fortunes of the lovely heroine. It is in reading anew, and better after the lapse of years, that one finds the evidences of the poet's power in the descriptions of rural life. When the mind has comprehended the pictures of peace and innocence, the sights and sounds of the farm-yard, and the fervent religious character of the simple-hearted people, it gives a sense as

of having lived in the fabled golden age.
One thinks of the landscape of Poussin with
its motto, *Et ego in Arcadia vixi.* The effect
of poetry is strongly cumulative, and the
power or beauty of detached lines is never
felt as it is when they are in proper place.
But a few quotations may be pardoned, if
only to renew old associations in the minds
of readers. The difficulty is in selection
among so many.

"Softly the Angelus sounded, and over the roofs of the village
 Columns of pale blue smoke, like clouds of incense ascending,
 Rose from a hundred hearths, the homes of peace and contentment."

" Homeward serenely she walked, with God's benediction upon
   her.
 When she had passed, it seemed like the ceasing of exquisite
   music."

" Now recommenced the reign of rest and affection and stillness.
 Day with its burden and heat had departed, and twilight
   descending
 Brought back the evening star to the sky, and the herds to
   the homestead.

Pawing the ground they came, and resting their necks on
  each other,
And with their nostrils distended inhaling the freshness of
  evening.
Foremost, bearing the bell, Evangeline's beautiful heifer,
Proud of her snow-white hide, and the ribbon that waved
  from her collar,
Quietly paced and slow, as if conscious of human affection."

" Silently, one by one, in the infinite meadows of heaven
  Blossomed the lovely stars, the forget-me-nots of the angels."

" Down sank the great red sun, and in golden, glimmering
  vapors
  Veiled the light of his face, like the Prophet descending
  from Sinai."

" Feeling is deep and still ; and the word that floats on the
  surface
  Is as the tossing buoy, that betrays where the anchor is
  hidden."

Space must be given for two quotations
more, as they show the profound religious
convictions and piety of the author.

" The manifold flowers of the garden
Poured out their souls in odors, that were their prayers and
  confessions,
Unto the night, as it went its way, like a silent Carthusian."

" Look at this vigorous plant that lifts its head from the
    meadow,
See how its leaves are turned to the north, as true as the
    magnet ;
This is the compass-flower, that the finger of God has
    planted
Here in the houseless wild, to direct the traveller's journey
Over the sea-like, pathless, limitless waste of the desert.
Such in the soul of man is faith.   The blossoms of passion,
Gay and luxuriant flowers, are brighter and fuller of fra-
    grance,
But they beguile us, and lead us astray, and their odor is
    deadly.
Only this humble plant can guide us here, and hereafter
Crown us with asphodel flowers, that are wet with the dews
    of nepenthe."

It was lately remarked that Longfellow
had fulfilled one important mission : at a time
when the world was in a ferment of discussion, and the old foundations seemed to have
been undermined, — when the hopes of mankind for the hereafter were darkened with
fears, — when the very Deity had nearly disappeared in a haze of scholastic definitions
and doubts, — it was for the poet to show the
true centre of gravity in the spiritual realm,

seen by faith and reason alike, and holding all souls by the attraction of love.[1]

A correspondent of the New York Times relates the following story as coming from Longfellow: —

" I got the climax of ' Evangeline' from Philadelphia, and it was singular how I happened to do so. I was passing down Spruce Street one day toward my hotel after a walk, when my attention was attracted to a large building with beautiful trees about it inside of a high enclosure. I walked along until I came to the great gate,

---

[1] This is a paraphrase from memory of an interesting brief address, by Prof. G. Stanley Hall, at a Longfellow Birthday Celebration at the School for the Blind in South Boston.

As creeds and philosophies decay, the poet has a practical and needful task in giving such expression to the emotional life as shall give poise and self-possession to the soul. Lotze pities those who try to *prove* God, soul, immortality, or anything beyond sense, — referring to the *Gemüth* as the only worthy ground of belief. We see in Longfellow a poetical view of the tendency of those who have said in philosophy that " the heart makes the believer," and that " religion is a feeling," whether of " absolute dependence," according to Schleiermacher, or of " absolute freedom," according to Hegel.

and then stepped inside and looked carefully over the place. The charming picture of lawn, flower-beds, and shade which it presented made an impression which has never left me, and twenty-four years after,[1] when I came to write ' Evangeline,' I located the final scene, the meeting between Evangeline and Gabriel, and the death, at this poor-house, and the burial in an old Catholic graveyard not far away, which I found by chance in another of my walks. It is purely a fancy sketch, and the name of Evangeline was coined to complete the story. The incident Mr. Hawthorne's friend gave me, and my visit to the poor-house in Philadelphia gave me the groundwork of the poem."

If there had been any doubt as to the position of Longfellow among modern poets, it was settled by the success of this beautiful idyl. Its popularity was great among all classes and in all lands. It was especially admired in England, and was reproduced in many forms. The artist Faed painted a picture of the heroine, which was afterwards

---

[1] Possibly the date is wrong, as twenty-four years before Longfellow was an undergraduate at Bowdoin College.

engraved, and is everywhere known. It represents her as she might have appeared when, thinking of her lover, she

" Sat by some nameless grave, and thought that perhaps in
    its bosom
 He was already at rest, and she longed to slumber beside
    him."

KAVANAGH.

" Kavanagh " was published in 1849, and proved to be the least popular of the author's books. The story is slight, but pleasing, and the few incidents are chosen and presented with a poet's art. But the mild flavor of such a novel hardly satisfies readers of modern fiction, which has become of late so intense and passionate. Many a classic would utterly fail of success if it were new to-day. Imagine the disgust at the circulating libraries if there were to appear a counterpart of the Vicar of Wakefield, or Paul and Virginia! The thing in " Kavanagh " which haunts the memory of every writer is the procrastination of Churchill, who, like Coleridge, imagined works that were to be done ; books with gorgeous titles that were always alluring him like the domes of Kubla Khan, but were never made his own. An author sees in this common experience how the petty cares, the poverty, the narrowness, of Churchill's life filched day by day his golden hours, chilled his once ardent hopes, and confined him in half involuntary inaction as in a prison, until he was borne to the resting-place where there is neither work nor device.

AGASSIZ.

The coming of Agassiz was an epoch in the history of Harvard College. If this institution is of late entitled to the name of University, the beginning of the change dates from the time when the great naturalist became one of its corps of teachers. The statement needs amplification. It is admitted, of course, that long before that time there were the post-graduate Schools of Law, Divinity, and Medicine, and that the Lawrence Scientific School had been established to afford a parallel *Real-Schule* course for engineers and chemists. The department under the charge of Agassiz was intended to furnish supplementary instruction in certain branches of natural history. That of itself would not signify very much; it was no single addition — though many came to increase the number and scope of studies — that raised the College to its present position. A second Divinity School was established under Episcopalian professors. Music was recognized among the liberal arts, and the new chair was filled by one of the most eminent of modern composers. A Museum of American Archæology and Ethnology was founded by George Peabody. The library grew, and its Gothic shell grew likewise. Appleton Chapel, new and luxurious dormitories, the superb Gymnasium, and the magnificent Memorial Hall arose. The force of professors, lecturers, and tutors was steadily enlarged.

But the change was less in these visible, material things, than in the general tone of thought and feeling. It was the case of an old-fashioned, quiet village becoming a city, and taking upon itself the responsibilities of municipal government.

Before that time single professors might count for much; and as positive forces and centres of influence they continue to count; but the great increase in the numbers and revenues of the College, and the coming in of men of mark, combined to make a total in which even the most brilliant specialists were almost lost individually. Men spoke less of the learned botanist, Gray, of the mathematical Titan, Peirce, or of the ardent Hellenist, Felton, but more of the combined power and resources of the University.

The effectual realization of the ever-growing plans of the College government was to come later, under the sagacious and brilliant administration of President Eliot,— a man born to rule, being far-seeing and bold, yet possessed of infinite tact and patience. We have seen how Harvard Clubs have arisen in the principal cities, East and West, with tributary zeal and loyalty to the Alma Mater. We have seen how the locks of strong-boxes have opened, as needs for new buildings and new endowments have arisen. And now it appears that no Boston millionnaire of liberal training can look forward to the quiet of Mount Auburn, and to such an obituary notice as he would desire, until he has consulted his solicitor and the President, and made a bequest for Harvard.

All this is recent; but the influence had largely begun during the time of Agassiz's residence in Cambridge. He was a patient student of details, yet possessed of the co-ordinating faculty which gave him rank among the great naturalists. But his power over men came from his large and genial nature: his was a sunny intellect, displayed in the most sunny of countenances, and by the most fascinating talk. There was no *nimbus* of reserve around his clear soul. He had known university life abroad as few Cambridge men had then known it. He had come to honor in all seats of learning. He had declined the senatorship and pension offered by the French Emperor, and had bravely chosen liberty (and poverty too, if need be), on this side of the Atlantic. The great-hearted — if somewhat prejudiced and grudging — State of Massachusetts became in a way his patron. The people were proud of him and adopted him, and raised acres of bricks to shelter his huge collections. He became an American citizen, and as thorough a Cambridge man as if he had the blood of the Quincys, Nortons, and Wares in his veins. He married the daughter of Thomas G. Cary, an eminent citizen of Boston, and so became brother-in-law to the Greek Professor, Felton. There was so much magnetism in his nature, so much power under his charming simplicity of manner, that he affected the Faculty as well as the students, and the people as well as the *savants*.

It is difficult to show the full significance of the change before mentioned. One feature was the gradual secularization of the University. A century ago a college professor was invariably "the Reverend" so-and-so. A clergyman, to be sure, may be also a chemist, astronomer, or philologist; but the knowledge of theology is not a prerequisite for the work of the laboratory or lecture-stand. And the most devout reader will probably admit that a faculty like that at Harvard, numbering near a hundred, composed of men absolutely first in their respective studies, is able to exert an influence upon the large body of undergraduates which no purely clerical circle could hope to equal. Truth, as well as light, has been polarized in our times: and though all truths bear a fixed relation, there appears to be no need of filtering the exact deductions of science through preordained funnels, or of imparting a theological perfume to eternal facts.

Religious liberty prevails at Harvard in its purest form; and though it is popularly considered a Unitarian institution, yet a majority of its students, and probably a majority of its professors, are not Unitarians. The one word which expresses the attitude of its teachers and the aim of the governing powers is the ancient motto on the College seal, VERITAS.

When Agassiz came to Cambridge, in 1847, he found Longfellow in the height of his activity and usefulness. A warm friendship sprang up between them. They were attracted by similar tastes and by common cosmopolitan culture. There was in the Swiss-Frenchman a breezier manner and more effervescence of humor, — in the American more attention to the minor amenities and social forms; but they agreed heartily, and they loved each other like David and Jonathan. Their diverse occupations established a pleasing and restful counterpoise. Longfellow would often take a look through the microscope in Agassiz's laboratory when at the seaside, and was deeply interested in the investigations going on. Agassiz in his turn enjoyed no recreation so much as an hour in Longfellow's study where the talk was of poetry and other literary topics. Either at Nahant or at Cambridge the pathway to Longfellow's door was the familiar end of his friend's strolls; and a week rarely passed in which they did not meet.

The group of "Three Sonnets" shows their intimate relations. "Noël," a charming tribute in French, may be likewise referred to; but the most beautiful of the poetical tributes is that written on his friend's fiftieth birthday, first published in the same volume with "The Courtship of Miles Standish": —

> "It was fifty years ago,
> In the pleasant month of May,
> In the beautiful Pays de Vaud,
> A child in its cradle lay.

"And Nature, the old nurse, took
The child upon her knee,
Saying, ' Here is a story-book
Thy father has written for thee.'"

THE SEASIDE AND THE FIRESIDE.

As we advance we are struck by the variety and fitness of the metrical forms in the successive volumes. Hardly any poet of our age has produced so many styles of effective rhythm. It is a common observation with superficial critics, and with the English especially, that Longfellow refined away the strength of his lines; and it is true of the earlier poems, that the finish and the dulcet melody are more remarkable than the nervous energy. But whoever takes the pains to examine finds that many of his subjects have been treated in bold, rhythmical forms, and that the lines move like squadrons to battle. Let any man of intellect and poetical taste read with due attention "The Building of the Ship," and then write, if he can, of

"lucent syrops tinct with cinnamon"! What
signs are there in this grand descriptive ode
of a refinement that has worn away the
nerve? The utmost directness and force
characterize every part.

The art that conceived and executed it is
like the many-sided art of the ship-builder.
We liken the two successes; and of each artificer we may say, —

> "For his heart was in his work, and the heart
> Giveth grace unto every Art."

> "It is the heart, and not the brain,
> That to the highest doth attain."

It is not only the technical perfection with
which the building and launching are described, — although the successive scenes are
as vivid as instantaneous photographs; it is
not alone the pictures of the woods where
the almost human pines are felled, stripped
of their green glories, and dragged away for
masts and spars; it is not alone the thoughts
of the beauty, mystery, and terror of the sea,
full of suggestion as they are; — all these are

parts, but the whole is more. The human interest speedily becomes prominent. We see the characteristic force of the old draughtsman, and the pleasing undercurrent of sentiment in the nuptials of his daughter and the apprentice. And meanwhile the skilfully wrought analogy between the vessel and the Union, scarcely suspected at first, grows, page by page. As the work progresses, we see what keel and what ribs are meant, and in the blaze of patriotic feeling at the end we see what momentous hopes are staked upon the vessel, and what flag it is that flutters at the masthead. So, after firm touches of description, with lively associations of coming perils, with a light breath of love in the sails, and with an overflow of sacred emotion that carries all before it, the noble poem comes to a close.

It has been recited by professional readers, declaimed by schoolboys, and quoted by preachers and orators, and still it remains the freshest and most stirring of our national poems. It may be questioned if any American audience (in the North, at least) ever heard it without giving the inevitable tribute of tears.

When readers come to the launching, they do not stop to consider the depreciation of the phrasemongers. The lines become alive, and the breath of the hearer quickens : —

> "When the Master,
> With a gesture of command,
> Waved his hand ;
> And at the word,
> Loud and sudden there was heard,
> All around them and below,
> The sound of hammers, blow on blow,
> Knocking away the shores and spurs.
> And see ! she stirs !
> She starts, — she moves, — she seems to feel
> The thrill of life along her keel,
> And, spurning with her foot the ground,
> With one exulting, joyous bound,
> She leaps into the ocean's arms ! "

It is perhaps a ridiculous comment at this point, but it may amuse readers to know that the late Mr. Hillard, who had placed this

poem in a reading-book for schools, was re-
monstrated with by a squeamish teacher on
account of the alleged indelicacy of the last
couplet.

The ballad of "Sir Humphrey Gilbert,"
like "The Wreck of the Hesperus," is full of
the ancient vigor, such as it was when the
language was new, and custom had not worn
off the sharp edges of words. There is not
a particle of modern prettiness in any of the
firm-set stanzas: —

> " Southward with fleet of ice
>   Sailed the corsair Death ;
> Wild and fast blew the blast,
>   And the east-wind was his breath."

Then we are told of Sir Humphrey: —

> "He sat upon the deck,
>   The Book was in his hand ;
> 'Do not fear ! Heaven is as near,'
>   He said, 'by water as by land !'
>
> .   .   .   .   .
>
> " The moon and the evening star
>   Were hanging in the shrouds ;
> Every mast, as it passed,
>   Seemed to rake the passing clouds."

To persons of impressible temperament "The Fire of Drift-Wood" is full of poetic association. The realistic opening, in the old farmhouse by the sea, in sight of "the dismantled fort," and of "the old-fashioned, silent town,"[1] disposes one to a sympathetic attention. The depth of feeling in the simple lines that follow cannot be paraphrased. Two stanzas may be quoted: —

> "The very tones in which we spake
> Had something strange, I could but mark;
> The leaves of memory seemed to make
> A mournful rustling in the dark.
>
> .   .   .   .   .
>
> "O flames that glowed! O hearts that yearned!
> They were indeed too much akin,
> The drift-wood fire without that burned,
> The thoughts that burned and glowed within."

In "The Fireside" will be remembered the beautiful and touching "Resignation," — a poem that has been read with sacred tears in countless mourning households. Memorable also is the thought of the "Sand of the

---

[1] Probably Marblehead, Mass.

Desert in an Hour-Glass." Observe the clear aphoristic lines of the first stanza : —

> " A handful of red sand, from the hot clime
>   Of Arab deserts brought,
> Within this glass becomes the spy of Time,
>   The minister of Thought."

This poem is very striking throughout, but there is no way to condense it, or do more than quote this specimen stanza. Others follow in this volume, remarkable for purity of sentiment, and for the rare tenderness in which Longfellow excelled all his contemporaries. It is an almost angelic tone we hear in them.

THE GOLDEN LEGEND.

In 1851 appeared this romance of the Middle Ages, and it is safe to say that upon no other work excepting the translation of Dante did the poet expend more labor. But as he subsequently gave a new arrangement, — placing this poem as the second in a trilogy, following the " Christus," and preceding

"The New England Tragedies," comment may be deferred until they can be considered together.

In 1854 Mr. Longfellow resigned his Professorship, and, as is well known, Mr. Lowell was appointed his successor. Longfellow was still under fifty, in perfect health, and at the height of his intellectual powers. But we know that the income from his books had greatly increased, and it was no longer necessary for him to go through the exhausting labor of teaching. The salary of a Professor at Harvard is one of the least advantages of the office. A competent bookkeeper or head-salesman in a Boston warehouse — not to mention the *chef de cuisine* of a fashionable hotel or club — gets better pay. Mr. Longfellow naturally felt that in seventeen years of service he had discharged the obligation, if there was any, growing out of his early appointment; and he desired to give the remainder of his life to purely literary labor. His relations with Lowell, only twelve years his junior, had always been cordial. Elmwood, the home of the Lowell family, is but a short distance from the Longfellow house.

Two persons more dissimilar could hardly be selected from a circle of men of high rank in letters; but there were enough points of contact in their common scholarship and their individual genius. The friendship between them was hearty; it was not the perfumed and placid civility of society, the display of which so angers a natural man; it was a simple, mutual liking. It is easy to see this in the poems which each has written for the other. We remember Longfellow's beautiful "Two Angels," written on the death of his friend's wife, and, later, "The Herons of Elmwood," of which we quote a stanza: —

> "Sing to him, say to him, here at his gate,
> Where the boughs of the stately elms are meeting,
> Some one hath lingered to meditate,
> And send him unseen this friendly greeting."

On the other hand, Lowell shows his frank and manly affection in a stanza of the

poem written for Longfellow's birthday, in
1867:—

> " With loving breath of all the winds his name
> Is blown about the world, but to his friends
> A sweeter secret hides behind his fame,
> And love steals shyly through the loud acclaim
> To murmur a *God bless you!* and there ends."

HIAWATHA.

This poem was published in 1855. The
light movement of " tripping trochaics," if
sometimes monotonous, is fascinating to most
ears, and the staple of the narration is wholly
new, at least to readers of poetry.

Mr. Longfellow made a long and laborious
study of the works of Schoolcraft[1] and others, and used the legends he found as a poet
should. That is to say, he built upon them
and adorned them with images and com-
parisons from his own mind. The primitive
traditions might have been more or less strik-

[1] " Algic Researches," and " History of the Indian Tribes
of the United States," by Henry Rowe Schoolcraft.

ing, but they undoubtedly gained somewhat by percolating through the mind of School-craft, and have been immeasurably raised in character by the poet's version.

The Indians of the Northwest were superior in mind and body to the native tribes of New England, but not greatly so. The substantial traits of the various tribes do not vary much. The historian of New England, with stern exactness, sketches the aborigines as they were, and makes havoc of their supposed eloquence and of their traditions. He says : —

" In ballads, songs, or some other rhythmical form of legend, most communities inherit some kindling traditions of the past. The New England Indian had nothing of the kind, nor of any other poetry. . . . . There has been a disposition to attribute to the red man the power of eloquent speech. Never was a reputation so cheaply earned. A few allusions to familiar appearances in nature, and to habits of animals, constitute nearly all his topics for oratorical illustration. Take away his commonplaces of the mountain and the thunder, the sunset and the waterfall, the eagle and the buffalo, the burying of the hatchet, the smoking of the calumet, and the lighting of the council-fire, and the material for his pomp of words is reduced within contemptible dimensions. . . . .

"As to traditionary legends, the beautiful verse of Longfellow does but robe their beggarly meanness in cloth of gold. Of what they owe to that exquisite poet it is easy to satisfy one's self by collating the raw material of his work, as it stands in such authorities as Heckewelder and Schoolcraft. The results of the 'Algic Researches' are a collection of the most vapid and stupid compositions that ever disappointed a laborious curiosity; but they were the best collection that, under the most favorable circumstances, was to be made in that quarter. Yet even of such poor products as these the mind of the native of New England was barren." [1]

So much for the material of the poem. In form it follows the measure of the Finnish epic, the "Kalevala," and like that poem, and like the Hebrew poetry also, it makes constant use of the parallelism, or repetitions,

[1] Palfrey's History of New England, Vol. I. p. 33 *et seq.*

which are so characteristic. One is surprised when certain critics mention Longfellow's adopting this measure as an imitation. By this rule every poem of our time must come under the same reproach. No vitally new metres have been invented for centuries. A poet takes the metre which he considers best adapted to his purpose. The parallelism is naturally employed, since it belongs to almost all the attempts at poetry in the early ages of the world.

But the resemblance to the " Kalevala " goes somewhat farther, and it appears likely that some dim remembrances of its more striking passages rested in the poet's mind. In the Indian legend, Wenonah, daughter of Nokomis (who fell from the moon before giving birth to her), bears a son, Hiawatha, to the West-Wind, Mudjekeewis. In the Finnish legend, the daughter of air descends into the sea, and there, made pregnant by the wind and waves, bears Wäinamöinen, the hero of the " Kalevala."

Hiawatha fasts seven days and prays God for the good of his people, and maize is given them in answer to his prayer.

Wäinamöinen sows barley, — the earth having borne fruit and flowers before, but no grain, — and prays to God (Ukko) for a harvest, and his prayer is answered.

The most striking resemblance, however, is in the description of the building of Hiawatha's boat. The reader remembers the passage, beginning thus : —

> " Give me of your bark, O Birch-Tree !
> Of your yellow bark, O Birch-Tree !
> Growing by the rushing river,
> Tall and stately in the valley !
> I a light canoe will build me,
> Build a swift Cheemaun for sailing,
> That shall float upon the river,
> Like a yellow leaf in Autumn,
> Like a yellow water-lily ! "

Hiawatha, we see, asks the trees for their wood, bark, resin, &c., and they speak to him in reply. Wäinamöinen sends a man to cut wood for a boat, who likewise addresses the trees and receives answers from them. The addresses and answers are, however, quite different from those in " Hiawatha."

Here are the addresses to the oak and the aspen as given in the " Kalevala." They have been purposely cast into Longfellow's measure and manner, as well as the paucity of the original ideas would allow.[1] The repetitions in the "Kalevala" are distressing to the modern reader, and the lines are difficult to render and preserve their primitive tone.

> " Then the oak he questioned, saying,
> 'Wouldst thou serve, indeed, O Oak-tree,
> For the skiff as mother timber, —
> For the keelson of a war-boat?'
> Wisely answeréd the Oak-tree,
> Gave to him these words in answer:
> 'Yes, in truth, to make a boat-keel
> I have store of wood in plenty.
> Thou canst find in my tall column
> No defects, no holes, nor wind-rifts.
> Three times in this very summer,
> In the warmest summer season,
> Through my leaves the sun hath wandered,

[1] Translated by L. U. for this work, from the German version, Hamburg, 1855.

> On my crown the moon hath shinéd.
> In my branches called the cuckoo,
> In my high boughs birds have rested.'
>
> .   .   .   .   .
>
> " Then he wished to strike the aspen,
> And to fell it with his hatchet.
> But these words the tree spake to him, —
> Spake herself, all breathless, eager :
> ' Man what is it that thou seekest?
> What desirest to take from me?'
> Then did Sampsa Pellerwöinen
> Give, himself, these words in answer :
> ' This I want; 't is this I search for :
> Frame of boat for Wäinamöinen,
> For the singer's skiff some timber.'
> Then most strangely spake the aspen,
> Cried aloud the hundred-branched one," etc.

This is the whole. A diligent search through the epic failed to discover another parallel mythus. The obligation of Longfellow to the "Kalevala" is small, — less than the obligations of many a poet. It is the prerogative of genius to build upon hints and suggestions. The poet, like the composer, *finds* many of his happiest melodies. However sacred the myths of " Kalevala " may

be to antiquaries, they are, like those of the
Scandinavian Edda, mostly absurd, trivial,
or monstrous. Taking the Indian tales as he
found them, casting them in the easy measure of the Finnish epic, adopting the parallelism which was once almost universal, and
with some hints in mind of which he was
probably unconscious, Longfellow has built
up a structure that is truly poetic, and as
truly his own. In his hands the story
becomes at once strong and delicate. The
thought is lifted up and illuminated. The
wigwam becomes a palace, and the Indian is
ennobled.

There is another curious felicity, that
while as a mere story "Hiawatha" delights
the unlearned, it has an inner beauty for
those who know what poetry really is. This
subtile and impalpable quality is shown in
many passages, wherein the words are simple, and their collocation in no wise unusual. The poetry is suggested rather than
expressed. When Hiawatha had struggled

with Mondamin, a demigod or superior being, he

> "Only saw that he had vanished,
> Leaving him alone and fainting,
> With the misty lake below him,
> And the reeling stars above him."

When Mondamin appeared again, he

> "Came as silent as the dew comes,
> From the empty air appearing,
> Into empty air returning,
> Taking shape when earth it touches,
> But invisible to all men
> In its coming and its going."

Among the specially beautiful passages
may be cited the last paragraph of the in-
troduction : —

> "Ye, who sometimes, in your rambles
> Through the green lanes of the country,
> Where the tangled barberry-bushes
> Hang their tufts of crimson berries
> Over stone walls gray with mosses,
> Pause by some neglected graveyard,
> For a while to muse, and ponder
> On a half-effaced inscription,
> Written with little skill of song-craft,
> Homely phrases, but each letter

> Full of hope and yet of heart-break,
> Full of all the tender pathos
> Of the Here and the Hereafter; —
> Stay and read this rude inscription,
> Read this Song of Hiawatha!"

Observe Hiawatha going for the first time into the forest: —

> "Forth into the forest straightway
> All alone walked Hiawatha
> Proudly, with his bow and arrows;
> And the birds sang round him, o'er him,
> 'Do not shoot us, Hiawatha!'
> Sang the robin, the Opechee,
> Sang the bluebird, the Owaissa,
> 'Do not shoot us, Hiawatha!'
> "Up the oak-tree, close beside him,
> Sprang the squirrel, Adjidaumo,
> In and out among the branches,
> Coughed and chattered from the oak-tree,
> Laughed, and said between his laughing,
> 'Do not shoot me, Hiawatha!'
>
> .   .   .   .   .
>
> "Hidden in the alder-bushes,
> There he waited till the deer came,
> Till he saw two antlers lifted,
> Saw two eyes look from the thicket,
> Saw two nostrils point to windward,
> And a deer came down the pathway,
> Flecked with leafy light and shadow.

> And his heart within him fluttered,
> Trembled like the leaves above him,
> Like the birch-leaf palpitated,
> As the deer came down the pathway."

The account of Hiawatha's fishing will be remembered, full as it is of brilliant, palpitating lines : —

> "On the white sand of the bottom
> Lay the monster Mishe-Nahma,
> Lay the sturgeon, King of Fishes ;
> Through his gills he breathed the water,
> With his fins he fanned and winnowed,
> With his tail he swept the sand-floor.
> "There he lay in all his armor;
> On each side a shield to guard him,
> Plates of bone upon his forehead,
> Down his sides and back and shoulders
> Plates of bone with spines projecting !
> Painted was he with his war-paints,
> Stripes of yellow, red, and azure,
> Spots of brown and spots of sable ;
> And he lay there on the bottom,
> Fanning with his fins of purple,
> As above him Hiawatha
> In his birch canoe came sailing,
> With his fishing line of cedar.
>
> .   .   .   .   .
>
> "Slowly upward, wavering, gleaming,
> Rose the Ugudwash, the sun-fish,

> Seized the line of Hiawatha,
> Swung with all his weight upon it,
> Made a whirlpool in the water,
> Whirled the birch canoe in circles,
> Round and round in gurgling eddies,
> Till the circles in the water
> Reached the far-off sandy beaches,
> Till the water-flags and rushes
> Nodded on the distant margins."

The aphorism which prefaces "Hiawatha's Wooing" deserves quotation : —

> "As unto the bow the cord is,
> So unto the man is woman,
> Though she bends him, she obeys him,
> Though she draws him, yet she follows,
> Useless each without the other!"

The dancing of Pau-Puk-Keewis is described with light and airy grace, but the passage is too long to be inserted here.

The singer, Chibiabos, is a beautiful creation, on which our poet has almost exhausted his infinite tender sentiment: —

> "Most beloved by Hiawatha
> Was the gentle Chibiabos,
> He the best of all musicians,
> He the sweetest of all singers.

> Beautiful and childlike was he,
> Brave as man is, soft as woman,
> Pliant as a wand of willow,
> Stately as a deer with antlers.
>
> .   .   .   .   .
>
> "All the many sounds of nature
> Borrowed sweetness from his singing;
> All the hearts of men were softened
> By the pathos of his music ;
> For he sang of peace and freedom,
> Sang of beauty, love, and longing ;
> Sang of death, and life undying
> In the Islands of the Blessed,
> In the kingdom of Ponemah,
> In the land of the Hereafter."

His artless love-song at the wedding of Hiawatha lingers in the memory. And when, later, the gentle musician dies, the whole forest world joins in the lament: —

> " 'He is dead, the sweet musician !
> He the sweetest of all singers !
> He has gone from us forever,
> He has moved a little nearer
> To the Master of all music,
> To the Master of all singing !
> O my brother, Chibiabos !'
> "And the melancholy fir-trees
> Waved their dark green fans above him,

Waved their purple cones above him,
Sighing with him to console him,
Mingling with his lamentation
Their complaining, their lamenting.
 "Came the Spring, and all the forest
Looked in vain for Chibiabos;
Sighed the rivulet, Sebowisha,
Sighed the rushes in the meadow.
 "From the tree-tops sang the bluebird,
Sang the bluebird, the Owaissa,
'Chibiabos! Chibiabos!
He is dead, the sweet musician!'
 "From the wigwam sang the robin,
Sang the robin, the Opechee,
'Chibiabos! Chibiabos!
He is dead, the sweetest singer!'
 "And at night through all the forest
Went the whippoorwill complaining,
Wailing went the Wawonaissa,
'Chibiabos! Chibiabos!
He is dead, the sweet musician!
He the sweetest of all singers!'"

Of all the touching passages in Longfellow's poems this monody for Chibiabos will be hereafter most affectionately recalled, when men think of the voice . that is now hushed forever.

"Hiawatha" was a novelty, both as regards

subject and form, and few men are able to judge of an entirely new species of composition off-hand. The poem was praised and ridiculed, and the feeling pro and con became intense. As we know now that the poem is one of Longfellow's best, it will be more entertaining, perhaps, to see what was said by those who disliked or failed to appreciate it. We copy the pith of an article from the Daily Traveller[1] of Boston : —

"We cannot deny that the spirit of poesy breathes throughout the work, ... but we cannot but express our regret that our own pet national poet [*sic*] should not have selected as the theme of his muse something higher and better than the silly legends of the savage aborigines. His poem does not awaken one sympathetic throb; it does not teach a single truth ; and, rendered into prose, Hiawatha would be a mass of the most childish nonsense that ever dropped from human pen. In verse it contains nothing so precious as the golden time which would be lost in the reading of it."

[1] November 20, 1855.

The publishers, Messrs. Ticknor and Fields, retorted by a curt note to the Traveller, withdrawing their advertisements, and asking to have the paper stopped.

The Traveller responded by copying the rather hasty note, and charging the publishers with attempting to influence the press, making their advertising patronage depend upon favorable opinions of new books.

This created no small stir; and as the poem· at the same time was attacked on other grounds, the newspapers from the Atlantic to the Mississippi were soon engaged in a general controversy. Through all this storm Mr. Longfellow remained calm, paying no attention to assailants or defenders. It is said that Mr. Fields one day hurried off to Cambridge in a state of great excitement, — that morning's mail having brought an unusually large batch of attacks and parodies, some of the charges being, he considered, of a seriously damaging character. "My dear Mr. Longfellow," he exclaimed, bursting into the poet's study, " these atrocious libels must be stopped." Longfellow glanced over the papers without comment. Handing them back, he quietly asked, " By the way, Fields, how is 'Hiawatha' selling?" " Wonderfully!" replied the excited publisher; " none of your books has ever had such a sale." " Then," said the poet calmly, " I think we had better let these people go on advertising it."[1]

THE ATLANTIC MONTHLY.

After the publication of " Hiawatha," there appears to have been an interval of quiet. It is not likely that the poet's pen was idle, although his motto as to his work must have been always " Without haste," as well as " Without rest"; but there was a period during which few poems appeared. The public bought immense numbers of volumes, but the magazines were not, as now, the munificent patrons of poetry and art. Something

---

[1] Correspondence of Cleveland (Ohio) Herald.

has been already said of the Knickerbocker and the Philadelphia magazines. Putnam's Monthly had a comparatively short, but brilliant and honorable career; of the purely literary magazines still existing, we can remember only Harper's that was successful then. But in 1857, and before that time, Harper's was largely filled with copied articles, and neither that nor any other literary periodical was an outspoken organ of opinion. It was then supposed necessary to avoid controverted topics, and epicene literature was mostly in vogue. Writers and thinkers might deplore this, but publishers were timid, and kept a weather eye open to watch the vanes of public opinion.

The Atlantic Monthly was started with the definite purpose of concentrating the efforts of the best writers upon literature and politics, under the light of the highest morals. Mr. Longfellow was one of the first persons consulted, and gave his hearty approval to the plan. The success of the new magazine is historical. There seemed to have been a wonderful accumulation of fascinating articles waiting for an outlet. The chief honor belongs to Holmes, whose "Autocrat of the Breakfast Table" was perhaps the most brilliant series of papers in our time, on either side the Atlantic. Much was due to the essays, poems, and skilful leadership of Lowell, and to the great name and characteristic verses of Emerson. And when Longfellow, generally admitted to be the chief of American poets, contributed a poem to nearly every number, the public had an assurance that the new magazine contained the best results of American authorship. Among the many beautiful poems of Longfellow in the Atlantic may be mentioned "Sandalphon," "Santa Filomena," "The Golden Milestone," "Catawba Wine," "The Birds of Killingworth," "The Children's Hour," "Paul Revere's Ride," and "The Bells of Lynn." The number of his contributions was large, and he was in his best estate of mind and body.

As the Atlantic was started at a dinner, it was long a custom for the editor and chief contributors to dine together once a month, on the last Saturday, when the number for the succeeding month was out. The attendance varied, of course, but the persons usually present for the first two years were Agassiz, J. Eliot Cabot, John S. Dwight, Emerson, Felton, Holmes, Judge E. R. Hoar, Dr. Estes Howe, Longfellow, Lowell, Charles E. Norton, and Edmund Quincy. Motley the historian came to the first dinner, "a picked man of countries," the finest specimen of manly intellectual beauty, probably, that our time has known; he left soon after, to pursue his studies abroad. Whittier came rarely. His health was always delicate, his appetite capricious, and he was evidently troubled by the clouds of smoke that succeeded the dinner. Occasionally Whipple and Trowbridge came; also, guests from abroad who chanced to be in town. Once only the women contributors were invited. The ideal dinner, as it exists in the mind of Englishmen and Americans, does not lend itself kindly to the refined tastes of the gentler sex. The experiment was not repeated. Agassiz was full of *bonhommie*, full of pleasant discourse, and was always listened to. The two brilliant talkers were Holmes and Lowell. Longfellow between them was "a sweetly unobtrusive third," and Emerson was sure to finish a discussion by some striking comment or poetical aphorism. Having read what has been recorded of the wit of after-dinner festivities of famous men in London and Edinburgh, the writer feels sure that the conversation of the leading men of this group has never been surpassed, and seldom if ever equalled. A reporter would have been a being to be shunned at the time; but what a delight it would now be to recall the scenes as they live in memory! The wit of Holmes and of Lowell especially never shone so brightly in print as in their dazzling but unstudied fence.

The dinners took place generally in the large front room at Parker's. Once the club dined at Fontarive's, when the host, a quaint and delightful artist in his way, produced a *menu* worthy of Lucullus. One dinner was given at Porter's, a once famous hotel about a mile north of the College in Cambridge, where the long-forgotten secret of flip still lingered, — where the tall and shrewd-looking landlord himself carved the canvas-back ducks and the mongrel goose, accompanying his masterly dissection with delightful old-time comment and anecdote. On this particular occasion the hilarity was general, — though still on the hither side of excess. Every one was in supreme good humor. The Medical Professor shone with an easy superiority, and tossed about his compliments like juggler's balls. Being particularly gracious towards Longfellow, and having just written that authors were like cats, sure to purr when stroked the right way of the fur, Longfellow, with a merry twinkle in his eyes, interrupted him with "I purr, I purr!"

The company broke up late, and on going out found that a foot of snow had fallen. There were no horse-cars, and all walked back to Old Cambridge, the younger members chanting Dr. Palmer's chorus "Putty-rum," from his East Indian sketch.

Mr. Longfellow continued his contributions to the Atlantic, as is well known, to the last years of his life.

THE COURTSHIP OF MILES STANDISH.

We must still use the successive books as milestones on our way. The poems which sang in the heart of the poet were the epochs of his life, and their dates must be our guides as we follow.

This romance of the Pilgrims appeared in 1858. The accounts of the trials and sufferings of the Plymouth Colony are among our most precious memorials; and perhaps the time may come when a descent from the first passengers of the Mayflower will count for as much here as a Norman pedigree counts in England. Readers must not confound Pilgrims and Puritans, — at least in Massachusetts history. The Pilgrims who came in the Mayflower had possibly got a little mellowed in Holland; not in doctrine, but in social life and manners. Judge T. R., himself a lineal descendant of Plymouth stock, avers that the Pilgrims played whist during all that dreary and terrible first winter.

The Puritans of the Boston settlement were as a body more learned, possessed of more wealth, and had left a higher social position behind them in England. But their bigotry was of an intensely bitter sort. Their literature may be seen in the pedantic and superstitious "Magnalia" of Mather, and in the mouldering poems of Anne Bradstreet. Their charity was exhibited in the banishment of Roger Williams, and in sending their most intellectual woman, Anne Hutchinson, out into the wilderness to be murdered by Indians.

Their jurisprudence is illustrated during the rule of the theocracy, when Cotton Mather and his fellow elders were as supreme as are now the twelve apostles of Salt Lake City; and when courts and judges, aside from statutes, based verdicts and death-sentences upon the five books of Moses. These things remain a charge against Massachusetts Puritans, and they cannot be blotted out by the tears of descendants; although the still visible groans of Sewall, the judge, in his Diary, dispose us to pity and palliation of his grievous fault.

The Pilgrims of Plymouth were more amiable; the milk of human kindness with them had not curdled. They had no quarrel with Roger Williams; they even sheltered Quakers. If we can believe the accounts of the time, the Quakers in 1640 were by no means like the venerable and lovely Lucretia Mott and the beloved John G. Whittier, known by us all; but were rather addlepated, half crazed by ecstatic visions, and by (supposed) direct converse with the Spirit of the Lord. When the Spirit of the Lord prompted people "to testify" by exposing themselves naked on Sunday in meeting, the Puritans may perhaps be pardoned if they attributed the inspiration to quite another source. This fact may serve also as a comment upon "The New England Tragedies" hereinafter to be noticed.

The Pilgrims, as a whole, were men of amiable manners and of noble character. Longfellow has grouped in his story nearly all the traditions that have come down to us, and has included among them some memorable sayings from John Eliot, the missionary to the Indians, who lived near Boston. The incidents of the return of the Mayflower, the plots of the savages to exterminate the little band of settlers remaining, and the valiant conduct of Miles Standish, are matters of history. So, too, has come down the story, which seems as if it were the invention of a playwright, of the sending by Standish of

John Alden to court the beautiful Priscilla in his behalf. The arch reply of the maiden is historical. The tradition of the ride of the bride home upon the back of the milk-white steer has likewise been handed down from generation to generation. If carping antiquarians query, and say that the Mayflower brought no cattle, and that there was not a steer in the Plymouth Colony, white, red, or brindle, that is so much the worse for them. Longfellow knew, as we all know, that the story ought to be true, and so he has given it. Therefore through the fragrant Plymouth woods and among its lovely blue ponds the milk-white steer shall continue to go without hindrance from us.

"The Courtship of Miles Standish" is more grim and realistic, less dreamy and poetical, than "Evangeline." The latter is an Arcadian idyl, the former a metrical chronicle. "Evangeline" is full of delicate sentiment, and its romantic idea haunts us like the remembered odors of flowers. "Miles Standish" tells us of stern trials and fierce encounters in the midst of scenes which we have no time or heart to admire. Nor is the measure of the Pilgrim story so full of music and changeful accent. Continually we hear in the martial hexameters the clang of Miles Standish's long sword. It is only Priscilla, the most natural and artless of women, who fully charms us, and makes us forget all else in following the story of her noble and womanly love. As we remember that her blood and John Alden's were transmitted to Longfellow, we feel a double interest in the woman who dared to let her heart speak for her. It was a beautiful thought of the poet, after more than two centuries, to go back to the Old Colony and lay his tribute of May flowers on the grave of the mother of his race.

NAHANT.

From about the year 1850 Longfellow spent his summers at Nahant. It may be of interest to readers, especially those away from the sea-shore, to give some account of this place; partly because it is unique and singularly picturesque, and partly because it is associated with many poems, and with the poet's seasons of serenest pleasure.

Nahant is a peninsula stretching out from Lynn into Massachusetts Bay. Geologically it is an island of granite with interior basins of fertile soil, connected with the mainland by a long and narrow sand-bar. The connection might perhaps have been sundered long ago, if it had not been for the solid road built over it. At the end of the peninsula one is practically at sea; at all events, the sea has its own way on all sides. The masses of rock around the coast are colossal, and they have been splintered by frosts, ground by icebergs, and creviced by eternal washings, until they form a series of pictures of utter desolation. In stormy seasons the roar of the ocean and the dashing of the gigantic waves against the rocky barrier are awfully sublime. A little west of north is Egg Rock, a huge bowlder carrying a small lighthouse on its back, like a candle for the returning fishermen of Swampscott. South by west, on a projection from the Great Brewster, stands Boston Light, a shapely white tower with a revolving light, showing the entrance into Boston Harbor. The Middle and Outer Brewsters are nearer; also Calf Island, Green Island, and the dreaded masses of rocks named The Graves. Due south stands the lighthouse on Minot's Ledge. Northward are Baker's Island lights, and, more eastward, those of Thatcher's Island at Cape Ann. Whether by day or night, in calm or storm, the views of sea and shore from Nahant are always fascinating; — sometimes as lovely as the scenery among the isles of the Ægean, sometimes as terrible as the storm-beaten coasts of Norway.

This small peninsula has long been a favorite summer resort for the wealthy people of Boston and vicinity; and, after those of Newport, its so-called cottages, which are elaborate and costly villas in fact, are the most picturesque seaside residences on the Atlantic coast. As at Newport, fashion for the most part has full control ; and the dress, equipage, lawn parties, and dinners are suited to the tastes and means of the rich.

Here upon a rocky platform, with a pleasant southwestern exposure, stands the cottage where Mr. Longfellow lived. It is a house of ample size, with wide verandas, and is surrounded with such shrubbery as the unsparing winds that sweep the peninsula allow. The season is short, beginning perhaps in the middle of June, and ending by the last of September. A few summer residents go nominally, or perhaps vicariously, before the first of May. Taxes are very light in Nahant, and in Massachusetts the first of May is the decisive time as to a tax-payer's legal residence.

Here around the coast, away from the few roads, perfect quiet reigns, interrupted only by the rote of the sea. To lie on the patches of grass in view of the grand rocks, and to see and hear the thunderous shocks of waves, or to look at the glassy, heaving sea, or to scan the distant passing ships, or the tiny sails of fishing-smacks, or to follow the manœuvres of the white-winged yachts, is a pleasure which only the experienced can value. Lotos-eating in comparison is a very nervous and unsatisfactory recreation.

For a long time Nahant was almost the only fashionable seaside resort near Boston. Of late the blood of the Vikings has reasserted itself, and almost the whole population flocks to the shore in hot weather. Enormous, gaudy hotels swelter on sandy beaches, or crown the green, cedar-dotted knolls, from Revere away to the line of New Brunswick. For three months brown hands and ruddy, tanned cheeks are fashionable; and young dandies are sculling in punts, while troops of masquerading bathers are gambolling like seals on the shelving, shelly shores.

The influences of Nahant scenery are evident in many of Longfellow's poems. It is true he came from a seaport town, but the Atlantic is at some distance from the wharves of Portland, and nowhere could he have felt the majesty and power of the ocean as at Nahant. Readers remember the poem "Seaweed," a marvellous piece of work, full of sharp lines to the eye, and full of remembered sounds of the ocean; perhaps as skilfully wrought in its imitations and assonances as any from his pen: —

> "When descends on the Atlantic
> > The gigantic
> Storm-wind of the equinox,
> Landward in his wrath he scourges
> > The toiling surges,
> Laden with seaweed from the rocks;

> "From Bermuda's reefs; from edges
> > Of sunken ledges
> In some far-off, bright Azore;
> From Bahama and the dashing,
> > Silver-flashing
> Surges of San Salvador;

" From the tumbling surf, that buries
    The Orkneyan skerries,
Answering the hoarse Hebrides ;
And from wrecks of ships, and drifting
    Spars, uplifting
On the desolate, rainy seas ; —

" Ever drifting, drifting, drifting
    On the shifting
Currents of the restless main ;
Till in sheltered coves, and reaches
    Of sandy beaches,
All have found repose again."

" The Bells of Lynn " is another charming piece, — a beautiful landward view from Nahant over a calm stretch of water. Other poems have clear references to the scenery of Nahant, which the intelligent will see.

A TRAGEDY.

Longfellow, as we have seen, had enjoyed a favorite's share of fortune. All his plans had prospered. He was the one person in Cambridge whom every one knew and loved. A quiet and studious scholar, he outranked all Governors, Congressmen, and other dignitaries.   Living in a university town where nearly every resident was the centre of some learned circle, he was, like Goethe at Weimar, the one man famous by divine right and by the universal suffrage of hearts.   If ever man had " honor, love, obedience, troops of friends," — everything to fill the mind with serene happiness, — that man was Longfellow. But the inner feelings of his soul and the sacred remembrances of love were locked and guarded from every eye.   Regarding these thoughts and their mementos he never allowed a word to pass his lips.   He might well say, with Lowell, —

> " I come not of the race
> That hawk their sorrows in the marketplace."

And for that reason, among others, the public have never known the inexpressible agony, followed by a chastened but perpetual grief, which he suffered in the loss of his wife.   It is impossible to exaggerate his devoted love for this noble woman, the mother of his children, who had made his home little less than paradise. On the 4th of July, 1861, she was burned to death in his presence. She was dressed in ample, flowing muslin, and by some mischance her garments took fire from a lighted match. The flame spread almost with a flash; the startled husband, seeing no other means at hand, seized a large rug or mat and attempted to roll it about her to extinguish it, but in vain. In a moment she received injuries which were mortal. His hands were severely burned in the sharp struggle. Nothing was left but the undying sense of his irreparable loss, and the image of a glorious soul to be treasured forever.

There is not, so far as can be ascertained, a single reference to this terrible event in his published poems. The world moved on, and the poet in time resumed his studies and labors, but there must often have come to him a thought like Tennyson's : —

> " But O for the touch of a vanished hand
> And the sound of a voice that is still ! "

THE WAYSIDE INN.

The "Tales of a Wayside Inn" have a flavor of Boccaccio, less the coarseness which the thirteenth century allowed, with some reminiscences also of Chaucer, first of English story-tellers. The expedient of gathering a well-contrasted yet harmonious company of scholars and artists as the ostensible narrators is obviously natural and convenient; it does not matter that it had been employed before. The scene is at the old Howe Tavern, in Sudbury, Mass., that had been famous for more than a century. It still stands, though no longer used for its original purpose. In the illustrated edition of Longfellow's Poems may be seen a picture of the tavern, representing a large and rather irregular building, with hipped roof and tall chimneys, surrounded by venerable trees.

In this ancient hostelry the usages of former generations remained with little change.

Open fireplaces invited guests to enjoy the warmth of huge wood fires; candles and primitive lamps served instead of gas; the table service was as unlike as possible that of the modern hotel; but the fare was substantial, and was cooked according to long-descended tradition. In short, the Wayside Inn was a sensible, comfortable, old-fashioned tavern, something wholly unknown to the present generation. The soul and centre of the tavern was the bar-room, where in a corner a portcullis and railing defended the mixer and his precious liquids. Hospitality, simplicity, and plenty have vanished from country inns, as completely as fireside comfort went when a " black pitfall in the floor" took the place of a blazing open fire. The pane of glass, with the

> " Jovial rhymes,
> Writ near a century ago
> By the great Major Molineaux,"

has been taken from the window and framed, and is now shown to visitors.

Among the *dramatis personæ* of the poems are certain well-known figures. We have no difficulty in naming the musician, Ole Bull, —

> "Fair-haired, blue-eyed, his aspect blithe,
> His figure tall and straight and lithe,
> And every feature of his face
> Revealing his Norwegian race :
> A radiance, streaming from within,
> Around his eyes and forehead beamed.
> The Angel with the violin,
> Painted by Raphael, he seemed."

The Sicilian —

> "In sight of Etna born and bred " —

was Professor Luigi Monti, an author, teacher, and lecturer, who was on terms of intimacy with Longfellow, and for many years was in the habit of dining with him on Sundays.

> "His face was like a summer night,
> All flooded with a dusky light ;
> His hands were small ; his teeth shone white,
> As sea-shells, when he smiled or spoke ;
> His sinews supple and strong as oak ;
> Clean shaven was he as a priest,

Who at the mass on Sunday sings,
Save that upon his upper lip
His beard, a good palm's length at least,
Level and pointed at the tip,
Shot sidewise, like a swallow's wings."

The youth
           " Of quiet ways,
    A student of old books and days,"

was Dr. Henry W. Wales, a liberal friend to the College.

The Theologian was probably intended as a likeness of the poet's brother, the Rev. Samuel Longfellow, although some accounts mention Professor Trowbridge, an amateur theologian.

We read, too, of a Poet,

        " Whose verse
Was tender, musical, and terse ;
The inspiration, the delight,
The gleam, the glory, the swift flight
Of thoughts so sudden that they seem
The revelations of a dream,
All these were his."

This was Thomas William Parsons, known to lovers of poetry as a man of undoubted genius, but of a nature so shy and retiring that he has shrunk from popular applause, and almost dreaded the clear light of fame. His " Lines on a Bust of Dante" are full of power; the compact thought, and the stern brevity that presents the naked idea and scorns all rhetorical ornament, are such as might have extorted praise from his illustrious subject. Mr. Parsons is best known to scholars by his translation of the "Divina Commedia."

"The Spanish Jew from Alicant" appears to be an imaginary person, needed to complete the circle by bringing in the thoughts and traditions of an elder time and an ancient race.

The Landlord leads off with the story of "Paul Revere's Ride." The fire of patriotism that burns in this ballad, no less than its rapid movement and its undoubted inspiration, will preserve it for generations. People who think of Longfellow as merely a bard of the proprieties, one whose nerve is refined away, will do well to read once more this vigorous, simple, and almost perfect specimen of art. It cannot have been a mere coincidence that this thrilling poem should have been written in January, 1861, three months before the outbreak of our civil war. We must believe that the roll of Southern drums had reached a finer and almost prophetic sense, and that the poet in this story was announcing to the still unsuspecting North the coming on of a struggle whose vast proportions and terrible slaughters were to make Lexington and Bunker Hill mere skirmishes in comparison.

The stories that follow cannot be mentioned in detail. We are glad to see in fair and graceful verse Boccaccio's pathetic tale of " Ser Federigo and his Falcon "; we welcome the bright and impressive versions of Talmudic and mediæval legends; and we follow the Norwegian through the Sagas of his fierce and slaughter-loving race. In rendering the latter, Longfellow has given us the leading myths and almost the poetic anthology of the Scandinavians.

As we pass, we must commend the noble thoughts and the high religious feeling shown in one of the utterances of the Theologian : —

> " And most of all thank God for this :
> The war and waste of clashing creeds
> Now end in words, and not in deeds,
> And no one suffers loss, or bleeds,
> For thoughts that men call heresies.
>
> . . . . .
>
> Must it be Calvin, and not Christ ?
> Must it be Athanasian creeds,
> Or holy water, books, and beads ?
> Must struggling souls remain content
> With councils and decrees of Trent ?
>
> . . . . .
>
> For others a diviner creed
> Is living in the life they lead.
> The passing of their beautiful feet .
> Blesses the pavement of the street."

The religion of humanity and the sweet charity of the Sermon on the Mount have rarely been more truly portrayed.

This series concludes with " The Birds of

Killingworth," a charming and impressive poem, for which the author will be held in affectionate remembrance by all who delight in the brightest and gayest of the creatures of our common Father. Among the minor pieces at the end of the volume is "The Children's Hour," a poem that will henceforth be read with a tender and almost sacred feeling by the admirers of the poet. What a picture of happiness, of yearning fatherly affection, this simple poem opens to us! Somewhat sadder, but even more pathetic, is the final poem, "Weariness," beginning,

"O little feet ! that such long years," etc.

The second series of the "Tales of a Wayside Inn" was not published until many years later, in 1872; but it may be briefly mentioned here as continuing the scene already described, with the same character, and with a similar variety of thought and music in the interchange of stories. The volume further contains "Judas Maccabæus," a dramatic poem in vigorous blank verse, and "A Handful of Translations," mostly from Oriental authors.

A third series appeared in the volume entitled "Aftermath," published in 1873. In this are some of the most beautiful of the whole collection. The story of Emma, the daughter of Charlemagne, and her student-lover, Eginhard, is charmingly told. "Elizabeth" is a quaint but genuine Quaker idyl, showing the heart of a delicate woman under the strict rule of the Friends. "The Rhyme of Sir Christopher" is also a poem to be remembered.

HAWTHORNE.

We have before mentioned Longfellow's early friendship for Hawthorne, and have shown how, with a poet's insight, he had discerned the signs of creative power, and the promise of fame in his early sketches and stories. The discovery was wholly Longfellow's: it was the clear perception of one man of genius against the dull optics of a whole generation of critics.

When Hawthorne's classmate, Franklin Pierce, was elected President, it was universally recognized as a proper and meritorious act for the new ruler to remember the friend of his youth. For Hawthorne was not a money-maker; that would have been wholly irreconcilable with the movements of his mind. He never planned an article nor shaped a sentence to win applause or to advance his own interests in any way. What rewards came he received, and until he went abroad as Consul to Liverpool, in 1852, they were scanty. At the end of his official term, as readers know, he went to Italy, where he wrote the most celebrated of his longer romances. He returned to the United States in the summer of 1860, and resumed his residence in Concord. His health had failed, and his subsequent literary labors were desultory and unsatisfactory. He died on May

19, 1864, and was buried in the graveyard not far from the Old Manse which his vivid genius has immortalized. Readers will remember the pathetic account of the funeral in the late Mr. Fields's " Yesterdays with Authors."

Longfellow has commemorated the scene in a poem of ideal beauty. We quote the last two stanzas : —

> " There in seclusion and remote from men
> The wizard hand lies cold,
> Which at its topmost speed let fall the pen,
> And left the tale half told.

> " Ah ! who shall lift that wand of magic power,
> And the lost clew regain ?
> The unfinished window in Aladdin's tower
> Unfinished must remain ! "

The small circle was broken. Felton, inaugurated President of the College in 1860, died, two years later, at Chester, Penn. Now Hawthorne was gone, and there remained Agassiz, Sumner, and Longfellow.

FLOWER-DE-LUCE.

In this small collection we see some of the most delicately beautiful of Longfellow's workmanship. It is perhaps some disadvantage for a poet to contend, year after year, with his own early fame. In the minds of most living men of middle age, the early poems had an established place; they had been often read and repeated; and now they were the half of an equation, of which the other was Longfellow himself. The new-comers were pretenders — to be scrutinized. Many have felt probably, as the author did, that, no matter how exquisite might be the feeling and how deft the art of the later po-ems, they could not, should not be admitted to take the place of those that had been as-sociated with so many thronging memories. In a sense, the old-fashioned admirers and lovers of the poet almost resented the thought that their spring-time favorites were to be overshadowed.

It is not easy to judge as to what would be the effect of the publication of such poems as " Flower-de-Luce," "The Bells of Lynn," or " Killed at the Ford," from an author before unknown. It is probable that they would be received with universal delight. Year by year Longfellow's fame had grown, until he was his own tremendous rival. From him great things were naturally expected, and a poem that would have created a *furore* from a new man was from him only an every-day occurrence.

This observation will be found to hold good, that whenever the reader sees any poem of Longfellow's of moderate length, — not being a translation, — it is sure to contain some high truth or some truly poetical image. It is in the longer and more labored productions that passages of less evident inspiration occur.

CHRISTUS, A MYSTERY.

The separate parts of the Mystery, "The Golden Legend," "The Divine Tragedy," and "The New England Tragedies," were written at different periods; the first named having been published in 1851, the last in 1868, and the Gospel story in 1872.

"The Golden Legend" (whose name only is derived from the "Legenda Aurea" of Jacopo di Voragine) is based upon an ancient German poem in ballad form, entitled "Der arme Heinrich," by Hartmann von Aue.[1]

So far as the vital idea is concerned, — the attempted voluntary sacrifice of her life by a maiden in order to prolong that of her prince, — Longfellow's poem follows the mediæval legend with little variation. But "The Golden Legend" has what we might call the stage properties, costume and scenery, together with a wealth of description

---

[1] Deutsche Classiker des Mittelalters, Leipzig, 1867.

and a richness of style which are all unknown in the German poem. For the beauty of individual scenes, and for the general poetical tone, there can be nothing but praise. The monks are treated in a most artistic manner, especially in the original edition. A few phrases which the poet's friends probably considered rather free have disappeared since. The entrance of Mephistopheles, of course, suggests Goethe, who reminds us of Marlowe, who reminds us of the prologue to the biblical poem of Job, — behind which we cannot go, there being no pre-Judaic traditions. But the notion of the presence and activity in human affairs of a spirit of evil is as old as the oldest of races.

For the mere pleasure of reading, "The Golden Legend" is a delightful poem; as a part of a trilogy it is fettered by connections on either hand to scenes and events, — ages before and ages after, — which are certainly not vitally necessary, if indeed they are not incongruous. A connection by a hyphen, a mere state of contiguity, is not enough. It is impossible not to see that many other events, such as the destruction of Jerusalem, the massacre of St. Bartholomew, or the martyrdoms at Smithfield, have just as vital a connection with the Scripture tragedy as have the monkish legend and the witchcraft trials. Having passed successively through the three parts of the Christus, it is as if we had gone from a primitive Christian temple into a dim and gorgeous mediæval cathedral, and finally emerged from a many-windowed early-Massachusetts pine meeting-house. The changes are shocks.

The story of the Divine passion in its original form can never fail of impressing the most thoughtless; but, so subtile are the threads of association, we find our thoughts and memories tied *to the very words* in which we first read it. A paraphrase or a commentary breaks the spell, as the fate of the new translation shows. The Gospel narratives have been received into the mind in certain clear, forcible, and often picturesque phrases; and they look fairer and sound more naturally in those phrases than they can ever do in verse.

There is an objection of a different sort to "The New England Tragedies," which must be felt by antiquarians and others familiar with the history of the period; although perhaps it may not occur to the general reader. It is that the several scenes are almost the actual chronicles versified; and they are terrible chronicles, — full of heart-sickness to the sympathetic reader, and tending to make him reprobate the Puritans and their jurisprudence, as beyond the pale of charitable judgment. Of the fidelity of the pictures there cannot be the least doubt, ·but therein lies the horror of them. Rather than read of Giles Corey's fate, and those other dreadful deeds, a generous man (son of the Puritans though he be) would prefer to pass a pleasant afternoon in the Morgue, and contemplate, under the cool, trickling water, the forms of those beyond the reach of man's inhumanity to man.

The objections lie to the choice of subjects as bases of poetry; and the difficulty in each instance appears almost insuperable. The language of "The New England Tragedies" is properly vigorous and condensed; that of "The Divine Tragedy" follows as closely as may be the words of the Gospel narrative; and these do not easily form symmetrical and firmly built lines, but resemble rather the loose piles of pasture wall, which are easily shaken when even a light foot trips over them. It is freely admitted that none but a true poet could have written either; the regret is, that, by attempting what is surely difficult, and apparently impossible, a rather mediocre success should be the result. The effect of "The New England Tragedies" upon the reader is depressing and painful to the last degree. There is no light, no relief, no escape from the fateful march of events. The Gospel story is finely harmonized from the four original narrations, and has many noble passages. Still, the feeling of stubborn resistance to any change from the early and universally received version remains, and will remain.

THE HANGING OF THE CRANE.

"The Hanging of the Crane" is a title that leads us to expect some rustic pleasantry connected with the beginning of wedded life and the responsibility of housekeeping. But the poem shoots swiftly ahead, and occupies itself with glimpses down the vista of time, which shift like the projections of the camera obscura. In successive scenes children appear, then new families, weddings, separations, and funerals. The poem is pitched upon a rather sombre key, and is not what a youthful poet would have made it, but is perhaps for that reason truer to human experience. The picture in the illustrated edition of Longfellow's Poems shows us a handsome and thoughtful man, engrossed (to all appearance) in a book, while on an arm of his chair sits one of those well-known aids to study and reflection, a lovely woman, whose graceful head is poised for endearment rather than for any close attention to the volume. It is a sweetly prophetic picture; but it is easy to see that the student will not make much headway until the scene changes. The lady might say, with Motherwell, —

> " Thy looks were on thy lesson, but
>   My lesson was in thee."

This poem was sold to Mr. Bonner, publisher of the New York Ledger, by the agency of Mr. Samuel Ward (so we are told), for no less a sum than four thousand dollars. The Ledger is not severely literary, and has only occasionally indulged in such luxuries; the last that we remember was the gift of ten thousand dollars to the Mount Vernon fund for a series of articles by the late Edward Everett. The prestige arising from the employment of illustrious contributors was perhaps worth what it cost. It appears to have afforded intense gratification to Mr. Ward that the price (by the rule of three) was not greatly different from that paid to Tennyson for some similar work.

MORITURI SALUTAMUS.[1]

The class of 1825 met at Bowdoin College on its fiftieth anniversary, in July, 1875. They were few in number. There were thirteen members of the class living, of whom twelve were present. Besides Mr. Longfellow, these were the Rev. Dr. Cheever, Charles J. Abbott, John S. C. Abbott, Hon. S. P. Benson, Hon. J. W. Bradbury, Horatio Bridge, Prof. Nathaniel Dunn, Rev. Dr. David Shepley, Allen Sawtelle, J. J. Eveleth, and a Mr.

[1] An allusion to the formula prescribed for the gladiators in accosting a Roman Emperor, when they were about to engage in deadly combat in his presence : " We who are about to die salute you." The venerable class of 1825 are thus represented as being about to die, and saluting their Alma Mater.

Stone, from Mississippi. The absent member was Mr. Hale, of Dover, N. H.

A friend who was present says that the scene was indescribably affecting. The large audience was hushed to silence, and the low and pleasant but often tremulous tones of Mr. Longfellow's voice as he read the poem were clearly heard in every part of the church. Of the former instructors, one only, Prof. A. S. Packard, was living. The meeting of the class was sad, but affectionate and tender. Mr. Shepley, in referring to this meeting and to the appearance of Longfellow as he read the poem, says: —

"How did we exult in his pure character and his splendid reputation! With what delight did we gaze upon his intelligent and benignant countenance, — with what moistening eyes listen to his words! Just before leaving for our respective homes, we gathered in a retired college room for the last time, talked together a half-hour as of old, agreed to exchange photographs, and prayed together; then going forth under the branches of the old tree, in silence we took each other by the hand and separated, knowing well that Brunswick would not again witness a gathering of the class of 1825."

To his class the poet says : —

> " Ye, against whose familiar names not yet
> The fatal asterisk of death is set,
> Ye I salute! The horologe of Time
> Strikes the half-century with a solemn chime,
> And summons us together once again,
> The joy of meeting not unmixed with pain."

The poem is a noble one, scholastic, as the occasion required, but full especially of the intuitive love of the heart. It shows the poet in an unwonted demonstrative mood, glowing with memories of his youth, glowing too with the inborn affection which learning and fame had never cooled.

Perhaps the final meditation upon old age is the most quotable passage : —

> " As the barometer foretells the storm
> While still the skies are clear, the weather warm,
> So something in us, as old age draws near,
> Betrays the pressure of the atmosphere.
> The nimble mercury, ere we are aware,
> Descends the elastic ladder of the air ;

The telltale blood in artery and vein
Sinks from its higher levels in the brain;
Whatever poet, orator, or sage
May say of it, old age is still old age.
It is the waning, not the crescent moon,
The dusk of evening, not the blaze of noon :
It is not strength, but weakness; not desire,
But its surcease ; not the fierce heat of fire,
The burning and cousuming element,
But that of ashes and of embers spent,
In which some living sparks we still discern,
Enough to warm, but not enough to burn.

．　　．　　．　　．　　．

For age is opportunity no less
Than youth itself, though in another dress,
And as the evening twilight fades away
The sky is filled with stars, invisible by day."

KÉRAMOS.

If there are evidences at times in some of
the later poems of waning power, seen in the
more sluggish current of thought, and in the
more obvious, less vivid forms of expression,
they are not in " Kéramos." The conception of this poem is very happy. We know
there was a rude pottery in Portland where

the commoner wares were made, and the poet when a boy often saw the shaping and firing of the homely pots and pans. Beginning with this simple experience, his fancy soon takes wing, and from an aerial height looks down upon the various scenes in ages past in which this plastic art has been displayed. We are shown ancient Delft, with its quaint plates and beer-flagons; Palissy at work with immortal fury to melt upon his wares an indestructible enamel; Majorca, Faenza, Florence, and Pesaro, with their wealth of color and imperishable beauty of design; the saints and angels of Luca della Robbia; the priceless relics of Etrurian and Grecian art; Asian and Egyptian images and vases; the porcelain of Cathay, including the nine-fold balconies of the tower of Nankin; the quaint and inimitable jars of Japan, covered with birds, and alive with all colors of earth and sky. These successive scenes are done with swift, bright touches, and form a moving panorama of one of the most fascinating of arts.

This poem was published with costly illustrations in Harper's Magazine, and attracted wide attention. It was afterwards collected with others in a volume under the title of " The Masque of Pandora, and Other Poems." " The Masque of Pandora " is a fine and nervous rendering of the old classical story, containing passages of uncommon power. The character of Prometheus will not take high rank, as compared with the immortal portraitures celebrated in ages gone by ; for it is not the remorseful or vengeful Titan that is exhibited, but only the wise and wary artificer, who fears the gift of the gods, and is deaf to blandishments. It is a kind of side-light upon the ancient story, told with spirit and grace.

POEMS OF PLACES.

Here may be briefly mentioned a work of magnitude, edited by Mr. Longfellow, entitled " Poems of Places." The series comprises no less than thirty-one volumes. The plan was to gather poems in English relating to various localities. Thus, under the heads of "Ireland," "Scotland," "France," &c., are collected whatever is descriptive of the scenery and historical events of those countries. This was a labor that extended over many years. Mr. Longfellow was greatly aided by Mr. John Owen, who was a publisher and bookseller in Cambridge forty years ago, and who was the original publisher of the " Ballads and Other Poems." Mr. Owen was a life-long friend of the poet; and his taste and careful scholarship were of the greatest service. His attachment to his illustrious friend was strong and constant, reminding us of the most remarkable stories in history or fiction. Mr. Owen was greatly affected by Mr. Longfellow's death, and followed him to the grave within a month.

A BOOK OF SONNETS.

This contains the maturest of our poet's thoughts and the expression of his noblest feelings, and may stand as specimens of his almost perfect art. The group entitled "Three Friends of Mine,"—referring to Felton, Agassiz, and Sumner, who had all passed away,—has been mentioned before. The characterizations of Chaucer, Shakespeare, Milton, and Keats that follow are strong and individual, showing a poet's insight and fine propriety of tone. As a specimen of the sonnet, that upon Milton is best, because it contains the development of but one grand thought, that breaks with a wave-like roll at the end. The others have, however, a remarkable vividness and felicity of phrase. In the sonnets following, "The Galaxy," "The Sound of the Sea," and others, the reader feels auroral flashes and mysterious emanations as from the infinite, and is excited by the tantalizing contiguity of ideas that attract him, yet baffle full comprehension.

These Sonnets form a magnificent constellation; and it would seem that, though late in order, they had been slowly evolved, and each luminous point brought out years before in perfect and steady lustre. If the early and popular favorites show the fresh heart and the unfailing melody of Longfellow, these sonnets as fully attest his vigorous mind and his far-reaching imagination. We insert two which are perhaps as striking as any.

" MILTON.

"I pace the sounding sea-beach and behold
   How the voluminous billows roll and run,
   Upheaving and subsiding, while the sun
   Shines through their sheeted emerald far unrolled,
And the ninth wave, slow gathering fold by fold
   All its loose-flowing garments into one,
   Plunges upon the shore, and floods the dun
   Pale reach of sands, and changes them to gold.
So in majestic cadence rise and fall
   The mighty undulations of thy song,
   O sightless bard, England's Mæonides !

And ever and anon, high over all
  Uplifted, a ninth wave, superb and strong,
  Floods all the soul with its melodious seas."

"THE GALAXY.

"Torrent of light and river of the air,
  Along whose bed the glimmering stars are seen
  Like gold and silver sands in some ravine
  Where mountain streams have left their channels bare!
The Spaniard sees in thee the pathway, where
  His patron saint descended in the sheen
  Of his celestial armor, on serene
  And quiet nights, when all the heavens were fair.
Not this I see, nor yet the ancient fable
  Of Phaeton's wild course, that scorched the skies
  Where'er the hoofs of his hot coursers trod;
But the white drift of worlds o'er chasms of sable,
  The star-dust, that is whirled aloft and flies
  From the invisible chariot-wheels of God."

AN ESTIMATE.

Whenever a poet of real merit is to be considered, it would appear necessary to make a new series of definitions, or to modify much that has been previously written upon the essence of poetry. Nothing could be more disagreeable than to read, as of late, that Longfellow was the "poet of the commonplace." It is true the critic made the statement with many qualifications, but the statement is itself a contradiction in terms. Poetry is the exact antithesis of the commonplace; it rejects both the thing and the manner. Poetry is the essence of thought, perceived or evolved by the imagination, and made palpable to the mind by fine intuitive suggestions. Poetry is necessarily twin-born with emotion, and never shows itself except by appealing to the sensibilities, as beauty, grandeur, terror, sympathy, love, or joy. The absolutely pure element of poetry even in classic poems is seldom a large part of the mass; much of the staple of verse consists of the grosser material medium which holds the whole together.

If the critic above referred to had said that Longfellow was the poet of common life, it would have been eminently true in one sense: in that his best-known poems are associated with the touching and sacred moments of ecstasy and of sorrow, and come to the memory of all men like airs from the land of the blessed, with healing on their wings. Upon the basis of universal suffrage Longfellow would doubtless be the most popular poet of our time, and perhaps of any time; for it is certain that his readers are more numerous than those of any poet except the Psalmist David. However, we do not abide by the decisions of universal suffrage, but by the consensus of the great body of men of reading competent to form a judgment. If the number of volumes sold were the test of a poet's rank, there is another who would come very near; yet no considerable number of educated men would consider that poet a rival of Longfellow.

On the other hand, it is possible that a man of even superior gifts and graces might be less truly a poet if he chose to wrap his ideas in uncouth phrases, and strive for obscurity. Longfellow somewhere says : —

"Some writers of the present day have introduced a kind of Gothic architecture into their style. All is fantastic, vast, and wondrous in the outward form, and within is mysterious twilight, and the swelling sound of an organ, and a voice chanting hymns in Latin, which need a translation for many of the crowd. To this I do not object. Let the priest chant in what language he will, so long as he understands his own mass-book. But if he wishes the world to listen and be edified, he will do well to choose a language that is generally understood."

If one were to discourse upon poetry with Robert Browning in view, what would become of preconceived definitions? Poetry might perhaps be defined as transcendent thought and exalted feeling moving in musical rhythm. But where is the music of "The Ring and the Book"? Only the most skilled reader can accentuate the lines with ease, and either a tripping or a leisurely grace of utterance is out of the question. Again, we may say that poetry is sometimes an expression of the sense of beauty in the presence of nature. What of this is to be seen in Browning? What apostrophes, what gems of description, what notes of joy, are to be quoted? There are subtilties and cavernous pitfalls of thought, sharp dissections of character, and hints of grand and poetical images. But the hints are seldom elaborated into those enduring forms which we love, and all the characteristics which we might separately admire are mere by-play in the development of complicated plots, the clews of which the most attentive reader will frequently lose.

The beauty of lyrical movement is seldom, if ever, seen in Browning. His poems in some respects are like the rough, hollow globes of stone called *geodes*, in which by a freak of nature crystals of quartz are enclosed like seeds in a melon. Without the geode is a dull shell of flinty hardness; it is only when cracked by the mineralogist's hammer that the glittering clusters of gems are brought to light. Great as Browning is, intellectually, the standard definitions of poetry must be modified before he could be recognized as a poet at all.

"Philosophical" poetry is, in a sense, a solecism. Philosophy, whether in the form of proverb or speculation, needs no music or measure. Proverbs are not necessarily poetical; Bacon's aphorisms surely are not. "The whirl and delirium of song," or even its more placid movements, are antipathetic to philosophic serenity. Philosophy can never be the food, still less the pleasure, of any large number. Perhaps five thousand is a sufficient estimate of the readers of Plato in any generation. The Essays of Emerson, full of high thinking as they are, and full of intellectual stimulus also, are sealed books to most eyes. In coming times, when men are lifted to the level of philosophic thought, it may happen that philosophic poems will take the rank in popular estimation which they now have among the few. But for the present we must consider poetry as it affects the large average of intelligent men. We must not set up our standard for the few high souls, nor yet lower it to embrace the greater number of those who are pleased with melody without thought.

Although the greatest poets are not modern, still, as a whole, poetry is progressive, heightening in qualities, as well as growing in bulk; and success is more and more difficult as time goes by.

As we look back, what faint gleams light up the alliterative lines of Langland! what wretched rhymes we encounter in the hurdy-gurdy verse of Gower! what meagre wit we find in the crabbed Scotch poets of the fourteenth and fifteenth centuries! Our language, it is true, has increased in resources, and grown more flexible to the poet's touch; but the general progress in poetry is as much in its essential qualities as in the external grace.

What is to be the future of poetry who can say? With the advance of knowledge, the refinement of thought and expression, the sense of beauty may be revealed to the mind in new ways. More and more we find poetry diffused through rich prose; but the concrete substance will not be exhausted thereby; poetry is not to be dissolved or dissipated.

The old forms will never return. The cold clarity of modern thought is not the medium for the visions of the Divina Commedia or of Paradise Lost. A contemporary Dante would wreak his noble rage upon the affairs of the world's surface, and not upon the dwellers of the under gloom. A new Milton would construct his aerial edifice under the visible sky.

As for the drama, it has ceased to have a literary character. The future poet, whatever he may do, will not write acting plays. The play has become nearly a pantomime, — an acted story with barely words enough to explain the situations. · Shakespeare's theatre was at once school, *salon*, literary exchange, and oracle. Our theatre exists for diversion, and a successful play is like a pastry cook's *méringue*, — the more unsubstantial, the better. Besides, as every one knows, the press now brings all thought to our homes, and we go to actors for wisdom and wit no more.

Neither will the epic return. The nearest approach in our day is in the Arthurian poems; but even these are separable, — not of necessity continuous; and, taking them together, we feel little of the *crescendo* movement, the up-gathering of force, which characterizes the epic cycle.

In modern poetry we see that the best effects are produced in efforts of moderate length. A poem is an enjoyment for a sitting. The exalted feeling which it is the work of poetry to excite is necessarily transient. The movement of feeling is swift, and at the climax the ecstasy dies. If we look for the masterpieces of modern poets, we find them invariably short. Even narrative poems are strongly condensed, and we find that "Evangeline," for instance, is as long as the taste of our day allows.

The principal quality, however, in modern poetry is the universal recognition of high ideals in life, even among the humblest, — in the doctrines of equality and brotherhood, — in the cultivation of tolerance and charity, — in short, in the inculcation of the true "gospel," or good news, of "peace on earth and good will towards men." In this way the scope of poetry has been enlarged, and its tone elevated immeasurably. Though the doctrine be as old as the Christian era, its appearance and its commanding influence in poetry are as new in this century as the spectrum analysis, or the doctrine of the correlation of forces.

Two great poets have been born in England. After them there are a dozen or twenty, perhaps, about whose relative rank men will continue to differ. When the name of "poetry" was new, it signified emotional thought, music, and rhythmical movement together.

The emphasis was literally marked by *feet*, and the measure was floated on musical waves. Now the triple ecstasy exists no longer. The emphasis is marked, and the music is heard by an inner sense. If the ancient idea of poetry were to be insisted upon, there could not be found half a dozen poets in a century. In our time they would be chiefly Swinburne, Shelley, Moore, and Tennyson.

Swinburne finds the once crabbed English pliable as if molten to his touch, and the music of his lines is as exquisite as might be that of a fairy orchestra. The airy melody of Tennyson's songs in " The Princess " has never been surpassed, — not even by Shakespeare. This wonderful music the verse of Longfellow has never reproduced; and yet its distinguishing features are pure melody and grace.

The poem measures the poet, and it cannot be as broad as humanity unless the poet is in himself a representative man. We recognize limitations in Longfellow, as we recognize them in all the poets for two centuries. We rarely find in him the thoughts that dazzle and strike like lightning; nor is he to be compared with some even of his own rank, in the sweep of imagination, still less in the intensity of feeling. The stream of his song has been

"Strong without rage, without o'erflowing full."

But his powers were rare, his studies and opportunities helpful, his sense of proportion and of melody exquisite, his perception of beauty keen, his sympathy boundless; and as he has addressed the hearts of all men he has been singing for over half a century with the world for an audience. It is easy to point out where he is inferior in isolated qualities to other poets; but he has a totality of his own, embracing many elements in which even greater geniuses have no share; and in the extent and diversity of his works he stands the peer of any. If poets like Gray and Collins are immortalized by the few gems they added to our literature, what is to be said of Longfellow, who has produced fifty times as many, — most of them superior in force and beauty to the mosaics of the one, or the classic odes of the other?

The treasures of the whole world have been open to our many-languaged man; the blossoms of every garden have yielded him perfumes; and now in his verse we have the aroma distilled from millions of lilies and roses. He who has done this is not soon to fade from the memories of men.

TRANSLATION OF DANTE.

The translation of the "Divina Commedia," consisting of some eighteen thousand lines, and filling three large octavo volumes, is an undertaking of so much inherent difficulty, as well as magnitude, that a man might be pardoned if he should regard it as sufficient for his share in the work of the world. Yet this appears to have been done within a few years by Longfellow, pursuing his invariable method of *Nulla dies sine linea*, and without interrupting his other varied labors. It is a most impressive example of the wise economy of time.

It appears to be admitted that a perfect translation — like the existence of two identical minds — is impossible. The difficulties have often been dwelt upon, as by Dante himself, by Cervantes, and by Dryden. To produce Dante's poem in English with the power, the allusions, and the beauties of the original, would require another Dante as translator. We observe that the Divine inspiration takes upon itself the mental coloring of the subject of its power: so that the Supreme Mind uses at one time the vehemence of Paul; at another, the gentle and touching humility of John. So Dante's great work is bald prose in Cary, more poetical but still rugged in Rossetti, terse and trebly-rhymed in Parsons, or literally simple and beautiful in Longfellow. A few paragraphs are quoted from the opinion of an eminent Italian scholar : —

" The directness and simplicity of Dante's diction require of the translator a like directness and simplicity. The difficulty of preserving these qualities in a rhymed version is such as to make such a version practically impossible ; and the sympathy of the translator is shown by his discarding rhyme for the sake of preserving the more important elements of style. . . . . The method of translation which Mr. Longfellow has chosen is free alike from the reproach of pedantic literalness and of unfaithful license. . . . . His special sympathy and genius guide him with almost unerring truth, and display themselves constantly in the rare felicity of his rendering. . . . . In fine, Mr. Longfellow, in rendering the substance of Dante's poem, has succeeded in giving also — so far as art and genius could give it — the spirit of Dante's poetry. Fitted for the work as few men ever were, by gifts of nature, by sympathy, by an unrivalled faculty of poetic appreciation, and by long and thorough culture, he has brought his matured powers in their full vigor to its performance, and has produced an incomparable translation, — a poem that will take rank among the great English poems." [1]

ULTIMA THULE.

This boding title must have caused a pang of apprehension among the poet's wide circle of admirers. Years before there was a similar shock when the great Emerson printed his "Terminus," and began his chant with

"It is time to be old."

Longfellow was gathering his last sheaves under a late autumn sky. The poems in this thin volume are few, but mostly memorable. By far the most noteworthy is the monody upon the death of Bayard Taylor. As Chibiabos in "Hiawatha" represented our poet as a singer, so with a few slight changes this would serve for a memorial of himself as a scholar. It is like a pure and perfect column of marble, faultless alike in design

[1] Professor Charles Eliot Norton, in the North American Review for July, 1867.

and execution. It would be difficult to find its parallel.

" BAYARD TAYLOR.

" Dead he lay among his books !
The peace of God was in his looks.

As the statues in the gloom
Watch o'er Maximilian's tomb,[1]

So those volumes from their shelves
Watched him, silent as themselves.

Ah ! his hand will nevermore
Turn their storied pages o'er ;

Nevermore his lips repeat
Songs of theirs, however sweet.

Let the lifeless body rest !
He is gone, who was its guest ;

Gone, as travellers haste to leave
An inn, nor tarry until eve.

Traveller ! in what realms afar,
In what planet, in what star,

In what vast, aerial space,
Shines the light upon thy face ?

[1] In the Hofkirche at Innsbruck.

> In what gardens of delight
> Rest thy weary feet to-night?
>
> Poet ! thou, whose latest verse
> Was a garland on thy hearse ;
>
> Thou hast sung, with organ tone,
> In Deukalion's life, thine own ;
>
> On the ruins of the Past
> Blooms the perfect flower at last.
>
> Friend ! but yesterday the bells
> Rang for thee their loud farewells ;
>
> And to-day they toll for thee,
> Lying dead beyond the sea ;
>
> Lying dead among thy books,
> The peace of God in all thy looks ! "

Longfellow's subsequent poems are few. "Hermes Trismegistus" appeared in the Century Magazine for February, and "Mad River among the White Mountains" in the Atlantic for May.

SEVENTY-FIFTH BIRTHDAY.

FEBRUARY 27, 1882.

The Maine Historical Society made elaborate preparations to celebrate the seventy-fifth anniversary of the poet's birth. The people of Maine, and of Portland especially, have a just pride in the fame of the illustrious man whose ancestors had borne such a part in their history, and whose youth had been passed among them. His recollections of his native city form one of the best and most admired of his poems. Bowdoin College claims a part of the renown of her favorite son. Her alumni among all the learned professions meet on common ground when his character and works are discussed.

The subjects had been given to competent hands, and the proceedings form a full and excellent summary of the poet's ancestry, of his early career, and of his enormous labors. The Portland Advertiser's account on the following day covered no less than eighteen columns.

The opening address was delivered by the Hon. W. G. Barrows. Mr. James P. Baxter read a long and interesting poem entitled " Laus Laureati." The Rev. H. S. Burrage read a careful account of the Longfellow family. A very excellent memoir of the poet's grandfather, General Peleg Wadsworth, was read by the Hon. William Goold. Mr. Edward H. Elwell, editor of the Portland Transcript, had prepared an historical retrospect of Portland, with bright and charming pictures of society and manners in the early part of this century. The venerable Prof. A. S. Packard, the poet's sole surviving instructor, gave a sketch of him as a student, and afterwards as Professor at Bowdoin. The Hon. Geo. F. Talbot read a beautiful and appreciative essay upon the Genius of Longfellow. The Hon. J. W. Bradbury, who was unable to be present, sent a letter.

Mr. Longfellow was too feeble to bear the journey and the excitement; but numbers of his relatives attended the exercises. Portraits and various objects of interest were exhibited, and Mr. Baxter, the poet of the occasion, as he concluded his recital, crowned Longfellow's bust with a wreath from Deering's Woods. During the day flags were flying everywhere, and the vessels in the harbor hoisted all their colors. It was a grand holiday, and business was generally suspended.

Such an ovation was never given to an author in America before. It was a deep and spontaneous feeling of admiration and pride that found expression in the simple ceremonies. Generals, cabinet ministers, and senators come and go; they have their brief season of honor and applause; but poets, like the serene stars, shine on for ages.

PERSONAL TRAITS.

The public are familiar with pictures of Longfellow taken at various stages in his life's journey, and it is not easy to add anything to the impressions which his fine features and thoughtful yet tender looks have made. But no picture of him of really high merit as a work of art has ever been made. The Lawrence portrait is admired by some, and that by Healy has fine points. The lithographic picture issued by the publishers of the Atlantic Monthly was undoubtedly a strong likeness as regards mere accuracy of lines; but to some who knew the poet well, and loved him, it was almost a grave travesty. Photographs are numerous, and many of them excellent. Mr. Longfellow said to the writer that the one taken in Portland a few years ago appeared to him the most characteristic. In his youth, and during middle age, our poet was noted for his remarkable taste in dress, and in the arrangement of his fine hair. Indeed, he gave to the last the impression of a perfectly dressed man.[1] Later, when the hair whitened, it was allowed to grow and to disport itself at pleasure; and it often made one think of the loosely piled crown of an ancient prophet.

He was of middle height, certainly not more; but almost every one who saw him for the first time thought him taller. An English tourist wrote of him as a tall man; but as in the same article he mentioned the gray stone walls of the house, we cannot set much store by his observation. The poet's mother in her description of her father, Gen-

---

[1] It may appear a trifle, although with regard to some men no personal trait is trivial; but Longfellow had his hats from the same maker for over forty years. It is not necessary to name the hatter: all Boston knows him. He mentioned lately his recollections of Longfellow's exquisite dress, and especially between 1840 and 1850 when the Fox style prevailed, introduced by Daniel Webster. He said that Longfellow in a dark blue coat with gilt buttons, a buff waistcoat and black pantaloons, and with a well-brushed beaver (it was before the days of silk hats), was the most remarkable person that was to be seen on Washington Street.

eral Wadsworth, says that he was not above middle height, but that " he bore himself so truly " that he produced a different impression. It is evident that Longfellow resembled his mother's father in this dignity of presence and carriage. Mr. William Winter's description is pleasing and picturesque : —

" His natural dignity and grace, and the beautiful refinement of his countenance, together with his perfect taste in dress and the exquisite simplicity of his manners, made him the absolute ideal of what a poet should be. His voice, too, was soft, sweet, and musical, and, like his face, it had the innate charm of tranquillity. His eyes were bluish gray, very bright and brave, changeable under the influence of emotion, (as, afterward, I often saw,) but mostly calm, grave, attentive, and gentle. The habitual expression of his face was not that of sadness; and yet it was sad. Perhaps it may be best described as that of serious and tender thoughtfulness." [1]

[1] The New York Tribune, March 30, 1882. The whole letter is extremely interesting, and gives a better idea of the poet than any that has yet appeared.

Rather too much emphasis is laid upon the expression of sadness. One saw in looking at Longfellow that he was a man of deep and tender feelings, but his habitual expression was far from sad. It was grave at times, but often lighted up with smiles; and the consideration for others, which always distinguishes noble natures, gave to his speech and manners an indescribable charm. His tact was intuitive and exquisite. He seemed to foresee a dilemma, and would not allow himself to be placed where he would be misjudged; yet there was nothing that suggested timidity or a sinuous policy; it was the manifestation of a wise, friendly, careful, and generous soul.

Mr. Winter recalls instances of Longfellow's genial humor, one of which may be quoted:—

"Standing in the porch one summer day, and observing the noble elms in front of his house, he recalled a visit made to him long before by one of the many bards, now extinct, who are embalmed in Griswold. Then, suddenly assuming a burly, martial air, he seemed to reproduce for me the exact figure and manner of the youthful enthusiast, — who had tossed back his long hair, gazed approvingly on the elms, and in a deep voice exclaimed, 'I see, Mr. Longfellow, that you have many trees; I love trees!' 'It was,' said the poet, 'as if he gave a certificate to all the neighboring vegetation.' A few words like these, said in Longfellow's peculiar, dry, humorous manner, with just a twinkle of the eye and a quietly droll inflection of the voice, had a certain charm of mirth that cannot be described."

He was very methodical in the division of his time. The morning hours were devoted to work, and visitors were not admitted until after twelve o'clock. Only by patience and perseverance could his labors have been accomplished. In him were happily combined two powers that are seldom seen together in equal poise. His first conceptions came like inspiration, and his first draughts of poems were done with exceeding rapidity. He allowed the first impulse to expend itself while he followed where inspiration pointed. But at that point, where too many poets stop, he had the power to return and go over the track of thought, condensing, amplifying, heightening; so that the poem, without losing its early and original charms, was wrought out in fair proportions, with nice gradations of tone, and given a melody that would haunt the reader forever. Although he could toil daily over his self-imposed tasks, and was able to finish a huge work like the translation of Dante by the daily accretion of a very few lines, yet it must not be forgotten that he had his seasons of eager excitement, — the glorious, painful travail of genius; and that in those supreme moments were produced such pieces as " Sandalphon," "The Warden of the Cinque Ports," "The Fire of Drift-Wood," and " The Two Angels."

Visitors were received in the south front room on the ground floor. This is a library, containing, among other things, the author's original manuscripts, bound in a long series of volumes. Books, letters, and papers are on all sides. Tables, shelves, and even parts of the floor, are covered. On his writing-table were piles of letters, — many of them unanswered; for the whole world during the last few years of his life seemed intent on burying him under piles of correspondence. He pointed on one occasion to a large mass of letters, over two hundred in number, and said to the author that the thought of them was distressing. He disliked to be considered discourteous, but to answer all those people at his time of life was impossible.

Upon that table are two famous inkstands. One belonged to Coleridge, and bears his name upon an ivory plate. The other was Crabbe's, and was given by Crabbe's son to Thomas Moore, and by him to S. C. Hall, who also possessed that of Coleridge. Mr. Hall, in 1872, sent both to Longfellow, to-

gether with Moore's waste-paper basket, by the hands of General James Grant Wilson. General Wilson has lately printed the letter which he received from Longfellow in return[1] : —

" Your letter and the valuable present of Mr. S. C. Hall have reached me safely. Please accept my best thanks for the great kindness you have shown

[1] The New York Independent, April 6, 1882.

in taking charge of and bringing from the Old World a gift so precious as the inkstand of the poet who wrote the ' Rhyme of the Ancient Mariner.' Will you be so good as to send me the present address of Mr. Hall? I wish, without delay, to acknowledge this mark of his remembrance and regard, and am not sure where a letter will find him."

The general impression of that room is fixed in memory as upon a photographer's plate ; but it was so crowded with objects of interest that an enumeration would be difficult. Every one will remember the crayon portraits before referred to, the fine bust of Prof. G. W. Greene, and the multitudinous books.

The real study was in an upper room, to which none but intimate friends of the family were admitted. There in one corner, at a window looking out upon a lovely lawn, is the standing desk shown in the picture. At that desk were shaped the glowing images that remain to us more lasting memorials of the poet than any which the grateful public shall raise.

It has been mentioned that on social occasions the poet was habitually abstemious, and his whole life was an exhibition of perfect self-control. It may be mentioned, however, that like Tennyson, and like Lowell, his neighbor, he was fond of the allurements of tobacco, and always offered his visitor a cigar. Pipes he was not partial to, at least within doors, but on his walks, especially on frosty mornings, he often followed at a suitable distance behind some laborer who was smoking a grimly colored " T. D." that Tennyson would have envied, and enjoyed the just perceptible odor of the peculiar thin blue smoke.

He was never really robust, although his natural vigor was sufficient to sustain him in his labors and studies; but his care for his health was continuous, and he persisted in out-door exercise even when it was far from agreeable. In the spring or autumn, when raw or blustering winds prevailed, he would wrap himself in warm garments and go out to walk, although he might do no more than pace along his veranda on the sheltered side of the house. His health was generally

Ah me! how dark the discipline of pain,
    Were not, the suffering followed by a sense
Of infinite rest and infinite release!
This is our consolation; and again
    A great soul cries to us in our suspense,
    — "I came from martyrdom unto this peace!"
            Henry W. Longfellow.

excellent, but for a few years before his death he suffered exceedingly from neuralgic pains. It is a remarkable fact that his sight was unimpaired to the last, and that he never had occasion to use glasses.

His handwriting was peculiar, but very distinct. We give a few specimen lines of his manuscript, which have been very kindly furnished us by the family for this purpose.

Referring once more to his correspondence, it should be said that his industry and self-sacrificing benevolence in giving counsel to young writers were commendable. His sympathy for the anxious aspirants for fame was inexhaustible. Nearly every writer of our time has borne testimony to this trait in letters published since the poet's death. Mr. Winter's letters have been referred to, but a very great number of similar tributes have been printed, which it is impossible even to mention. Such a mass of letters, with anecdotes and traits, have appeared, that it would not be difficult to make a kind of Longfellow biography by the aid of a little industry and a pair of scissors.

There are things, however, not known to the public; and as in some instances they concern persons lately deceased or still living, they cannot now be mentioned, except in a general way. His personal charities were constant and large in amount. Many an author and artist has received not only unsolicited sympathy, but a substantial check in his hour of need. There are persons who will read this with grateful recollections and tears.

Say what we will, the personality of a poet is an inevitable element of his fame. And proud as we may be of Longfellow's merited renown, we have an added respect and admiration growing out of his pure and noble life, his thoughtful kindness, and his unobtrusive benevolence. So that it may be doubted if the passing away of any of the great masters of our English speech would have made so deep an impression, or left such a void in the world.

There is little room to mention the honors received, or the illustrious visitors entertained by the poet. Foreigners of distinction were always taken to see him and his historic residence. Among the latest were the descendants of Counts Rochambeau and De Grasse, and the Emperor of Brazil. He was an honorary member of numerous learned societies. In 1859 Harvard College conferred upon him the degree of LL. D. In June, 1868, the University of Cambridge in England made him D. C. L. On the 4th of July in the same year he visited the Queen at Windsor, by command; and his reception is said to have been most cordial. In July, 1869, the University of Oxford also conferred upon him the title of D. C. L.

Throughout the Canadian provinces Longfellow has been honored as much as if he were a subject of their Queen. In Nova Scotia the regard for him is especially strong;

if the canonization of a poet were possible, he would be the patron saint of the Acadian peninsula. In Montreal and Quebec there seems to be no notion of a boundary line in literature. The sympathies of the writers in those cities have reached over to us; and their touching articles since Longfellow's death have made us feel more intensely the pulsation of the common blood in our veins.[1]

LAST HOURS.

During several years past Mr. Longfellow's health was a matter of some solicitude to himself and friends. His eyes had not lost their lustre, and his voice was clear and steady; but there was a sense of insecurity, though for no very apparent reason. He had suffered severely, often excruciatingly, from neuralgic pains, sometimes in the form of sciatica; and later he had been threatened with

---

[1] See in the Quebec Morning Chronicle for March 25, 1882, a warm-hearted and able article by Mr. George Stewart, Jr.

a still more formidable malady, from which he recovered. The writer saw him two weeks before his death, and well remembers his light and active step, his beaming countenance and cheery voice. He had not seemed in better health for years. The shadow of the last enemy had not fallen upon him. But in a few days the news was given out that he was seriously ill with peritonitis, and the daily bulletins had an ominous tone. He sank rapidly, and on the 24th of March, at a quarter past three P. M., he expired. His family and near relatives were with him.

He was buried on Sunday, the 26th. There was a simple service at the house, conducted by the brother of the deceased, the Rev. Samuel Longfellow, in the presence of the family and a very few intimate friends. Among the latter were Ralph Waldo Emerson, who has since died, Oliver Wendell Holmes, George William Curtis, Charles Eliot Norton, and George W. Greene.

The body was carried to Mount Auburn

Cemetery, and placed in his proprietary lot, on Indian Ridge, not far from the entrance.

A memorial service was held later in the day in Appleton Chapel, in the College grounds, at which an immense audience was present. The family shrank from having a public funeral; but if it could have been allowed, multitudes would have availed themselves of the sad privilege of looking once more upon the venerated face.

As has been said before, the newspapers were filled with accounts of the dead poet. Elaborate biographies and critical estimates, with letters and anecdotes, were printed throughout the United States and Great Britain. Such universal interest has seldom, if ever, been shown. And it is certain that the demise of no living man would cause such wide-spread and lasting grief.

The citizens of Cambridge have already taken measures to place a memorial statue near the house in which he lived, in an open field extending towards the Charles, the prospect of which he dearly loved and often sung.

After the natural tears at parting, there could be no regret felt for the close of such a perfect and well-rounded life. From boyhood he had borne his part, and had been faithful to the talents intrusted to him. His life had been not only without stain, but without shadow; it was a life that shone with a light like that of the blessed; it was a life full of toil, but crowned with honor and with the full fruition of his hopes; it was a life hallowed by the purest affection, by the sweet solace of children, by the devoted love of friends, by the reverent respect of fellow-citizens and neighbors, and by the absolute worship of humble dependents, who knew his open and generous heart.

He had accomplished a vast work, which had filled out the whole of his allotted time. He could have had little to regret; and having reached a period when, according to the Psalmist, the continuance of his strength would be only "labor and sorrow," he could calmly resign himself to the last great change, sustained by an immortal hope.

In coming times the lover of poetry, as he visits Cambridge, will regard the poet's grave as a holy spot. The grand old house, let us hope, will remain as he left it, as long as Time shall spare it. And the sculptor will mould in bronze his venerated form and noble features in classic and enduring grace, so that something like his presence may be seen to overlook the beautiful landscape.

APPENDIX.

No. I.

ADDRESS OF THE HON. W. G. BARROWS, OF BRUNSWICK.

I BELIEVE it to be a part of my pleasant duty to state the object of our meeting.

The first notice of it which I saw in the newspapers mentioned it, if I remember rightly, as a meeting to do honor to the poet Longfellow on the occasion of his seventy-fifth birthday. Perhaps it would be more accurate to say that it is a meeting to testify our sense of the honor he has done to this, his birthplace. It is very little we can do to honor him whose own works have long ago crowned him a king in the hearts of men, to bear sway wherever and so long as the English language is spoken or understood.

18

We meet to claim for this good city the honor which from time immemorial has always been conceded to the birthplaces of poets and seers, —. to do our part to link the name of "the dear old town" with his, as he has linked it in the loving description which he has given in the idyl of "My Lost Youth."

For a more potent reason than the chiselled inscription on the ancient mill which links the name of Oliver Basselin with the Valley of the Vire, in all coming time, shall "the poet's memory here of the landscape make a part," because we know that the lyrics of *our* poet *are* indeed

> "Songs of that high art
> Which, as winds do in the pine,
> Find an answer in each heart,"

and we want to bear witness to this.

More than this, we meet to testify our sense of personal obligation to him, not merely for the exquisite pleasure afforded by the wonderful melody of his verse, but for the didactic force that has impressed it on us that

> "All common things, each day's events,
> That with the hour begin and end,
> Our pleasures and our discontents,
> Are rounds by which we may ascend."

It is no mere gospel of idle contentment with pleasant trifles that he has preached to us.   Even the dullest of us could not read him without being moved at least to strive to place ourselves on a higher plane, — Excelsior! In ancient days poet and seer were convertible terms, and the best of our modern poets are prophets also. What insight was it which made him, in January, 1861, rouse us with

> "Listen, my children, and you shall hear
> Of the midnight ride of Paul Revere,"

when all unconsciously we stood so near another and bloodier Lexington?

Philanthropy of the purest, patriotism of the most exalted kind have by turns inspired him; and whether he sings of the Slave's Dream, or the Warning of

> "The poor blind Samson in this land
> Shorn of his strength and bound in bonds of steel,"

or of the Cumberland sunk in Hampton Roads, or of the beautiful youth slain at the ford, the lesson was timely, and it told the story well of the heroism and endurance which carried this nation through its last great struggle triumphant. We meet to pass an hour in expressing our admiration for the bard, the scholar, and the patriot, since every utterance from his youth up has been fine and noble, and has tended to raise this nation in the scale of humanity. I am proud to say that when he lived with us he was an active member of this society, and the ripe and golden fruits of his historical studies we have in the story of Priscilla the Puritan maiden, in the pensive loveliness of Evangeline, that tale of the " strength, submission and patience " of the Acadian refugees, and in the musical song of Hiawatha, and many another gem set in tuneful verse. But after all it seems to me that that which brings him nearer to our hearts, and has more to do with bringing us together here to-night than his wide-spread renown or the fame that attaches to his more stately and elaborate poems, is the light which he has thrown around home and hearth and heart in some of those lighter but unequalled lyrics which from time to time have " gone through us with a thrill," — which are haunting our memories still, and which are and will always be dear to us because dear to those whom we love. Who of us can think of home, now, and all that we hold dear in it, without somehow associating with it and them reminiscences of the. Footsteps of Angels, the Golden Milestone, the Old Clock on the Stairs, the Children's Hour, the Fire of Drift-Wood, the Wind over the Chimney, and Daybreak, and Twilight, and the Curfew, and the Psalm, and the Goblet of Life, and the Reaper and the Flowers? And where can I stop, having begun to enumerate?

For nearly thirty years I have occupied the house he lived in when in Brunswick, — an old house whose first proprietors have long since passed away, — and I sometimes wonder whether it is, in his thought, one of the Haunted Houses

> "Through whose open doors
> The harmless phantoms on their errands glide,
> With feet that make no sound upon the floors."

Since the wonderful legend of Sandalphon first made a lodgment in my memory, more than a score of years ago, I cannot number the times I have been called upon to repeat it in the stillness of the evening hour, and in the weary night watches, because its melodious numbers had in them a spell "to quiet the fever and pain" of one who has now for years breathed the fragrance that is "wafted through the streets of the city immortal." And hence it is that "the legend I feel is a part of the hunger and thirst of the heart," and my warmest gratitude goes forth to him who ministered comfort to the invalid in the sweet strains that breathe unwavering faith and trust in the good All-Father. Hence I say that we meet here to express, not simply our admiration of the poet, our sense of obligation to the teacher, the patriot and philanthropist, but also our reverent affection for the man who has done so much to brighten and cheer not only our own lives, but the lives of them we love, in sickness and in health.

Not he the poet of despair, or morbid melancholy, or depressing doubt, misbegotten by the wild self-conceit which assumes that the finite human intellect is capable of penetrating *all* mysteries because it has mastered *some*, and madly argues that it is a proof of superior wisdom to reject everything it cannot understand. Not so he, but the part of a broad Christian faith and an unfading hope that " what we know not now, we shall know hereafter," if we strive in earnest to rise above " that which is of the earth, earthy."

I think his motto in all his productions must have been, " *Nec satis est pulchra esse poemata — dulcia sunto.*"

> " 'T is not enough a poem's finely writ,
>   It must affect and captivate the soul."

If success can be predicated of any mortal life, surely his has been a success.

The Maine Historical Society and their guests assembled at his birthplace to celebrate the birthday of their former member, the renowned poet Longfellow, send him their fervent and united wishes for his health and happiness.

MEMOIR OF GENERAL PELEG WADSWORTH, BY THE
HON. WILLIAM GOOLD, OF WINDHAM.

The pleasant duty assigned to me for this occasion is to trace the origin and history of General Wadsworth, the maternal grandfather of Henry Wadsworth Longfellow, — he who had the military oversight of our frontier District of Maine, immediately after it was found that the British lodgment at Bagaduce in 1779 was intended to be permanent.

Peleg Wadsworth was the son of Deacon Peleg Wadsworth of Duxbury, Massachusetts, and the fifth in descent from Christopher Wadsworth, who came from England and settled in that town previously to 1632, and whose known descendants in the United States are now numbered by thousands.

Peleg Wadsworth, Jr. was born at Duxbury, May 6, 1748. He graduated at Harvard College in the class of 1769, which numbered thirty-nine, and included several honorable names, which added lustre to the class. One of these was Theophilus Parsons, who came to Falmouth as a school-teacher in 1770, and studied law with Theophilus Bradbury; but the Revolutionary troubles drove him away, and he became Chief Justice of the Massachusetts Supreme Court. Another member of the class was Alexander Scammell, also of Duxbury, who, after a brilliant career in the American army, received an inhuman wound after being taken prisoner at the siege of York-town, of which he died a month after. Both Wadsworth and Scammell after graduation taught school at Plymouth. In 1772 Wadsworth married Elizabeth Bartlett of that town. Their children, through their mother and grandmother Wadsworth, who was Susanna Sampson, inherited the blood of five of the Mayflower pilgrims, including Elder Brewster and Captain John Alden.

Immediately after the outrage at Lexington, Peleg Wadsworth raised a company of minute-men in the Old Colony, of which the Continental Congress commissioned him Captain in September, 1775. He was engineer under General Thomas in laying out the defences of Roxbury in 1776. He was in Colonel Catton's regiment, which formed a part of a detachment which was ordered to throw up intrenchments on Dorchester Heights, and was appointed Aid to General Ward when the heights were occupied in March. These works compelled Howe's fleet to leave Boston in haste. In 1778 Wadsworth was appointed Adjutant-General of his State.

In 1779 the British naval and army officers at

Halifax became sensible that they were suffering from American privateers which frequented the Penobscot waters, owing to their perfect knowledge of the numerous coves and harbors which they could run into at any time to avoid the British cruisers.

The Admiral in command foresaw the advantage that would be gained by establishing a naval and military post in this quarter as a harbor of refuge for ships and fugitive Loyalists, and to command the near coast and harbor, from whence they could obtain a supply of some kinds of ship-timber for the Royal dockyard at Halifax. This was the year after the French king had assumed our quarrel with the mother country, and had sent the large fleet and army to our assistance which gave the Colonies confidence, and made them more aggressive.

In June, 1779, it was decided at Halifax to send General McLane with a fleet to occupy Bagaduce, as the harbor best situated for their purpose. He arrived on the 12th of June, with nine hundred troops and eight or nine vessels, all less than a frigate, under the command of Captain Henry Mowatt, who had become detestable to all Americans by his cruel burning of old Falmouth four years previous. The people of Maine appealed to the General Court of Massachusetts for protection, and to have the invaders driven off by an immediate expedition before they could have time to complete their works of defence. The Massachusetts Board of War were instructed by the Legislature to collect a fleet, State and national, and, if necessary, to impress any private armed vessels in the harbors of the State into their service, under the promise of fair compensation for all losses and detention. The executive department of the Province was then composed of the Council,— there was no State Governor until the next year. The Council ordered Brigadier-Generals Thompson of Cumberland and Cushing of Lincoln to detach severally six hundred men from each of their brigades, and form them into two regiments. General Frost of York was directed to detail three hundred men from his brigade for a reinforcement, if needed.

The fleet consisted of nineteen armed vessels, carrying 344 guns, and convoying twenty-four transports. The flag-ship was the new Continental frigate Warren. Of the others, nine were ships, six brigs, and three sloops. The command of the fleet was intrusted to Richard Saltonstall of Connecticut, an officer of some naval experience. One hundred Massachusetts artillerists were embarked at Boston under their former commander, Lieut.-Col. Paul Revere,— he who carried the news to Hancock and Adams at Lexington that the British troops were on the road from Boston in 1775. The command of the land forces was given to Solomon Lovell, of Weymouth, Mass., the brigadier-general of the militia of Suffolk, which then included Norfolk County. He was a man of courage, but no war experience. Peleg Wadsworth, then Adjutant-General of Massachusetts, was the second in command. He had seen some service on Dorchester Heights during the siege of Boston and in other places. The ordnance was intrusted to the command of Colonel Revere.

The Cumberland County regiment was under the command of Colonel Mitchell, of North Yarmouth. The expedition was popular, and the people engaged in it with alacrity and zeal. Falmouth and Cape Elizabeth contributed a company each, consisting of volunteers from the most respectable families.

Under date of June 20, Parson Smith of Falmouth records, " People are everywhere in this State spiritedly appearing in the intended expedition to Penobscot in pursuit of the British fleet and army there." This was a State expedition, for which Massachusetts advanced fifty thousand pounds.

When the fleet was ready to sail from Townshend, now Boothbay, the place of rendezvous, General Lovell's land forces numbered less than one thousand men, who had been paraded together only once, — then at Boothbay. They were raw militia who had seen no former service, except, perhaps, some individuals who had been in the Continental army for a short time. It was a spirited body of men. Their fathers had been at the siege of Louisburg thirty years before. In one month from the commencement to organize the expedition it made its appearance in Penobscot Bay.

The British commander heard of the American fleet four days before its arrival, and worked night and day to render his fortifications defensible, yet it was far from being completed. He at once despatched a vessel to Halifax, asking for assistance. On the 28th of July, after waiting two days for a calm, our vessels were drawn up in line of battle, and two hundred militiamen and two hundred marines were landed. The best landing-places were exposed to Mowatt's guns, and no landing could be effected except on the western side, which was a precipice 150 feet high, and very steep. This was guarded by a line of the enemy posted on the summit, who opened a brisk fire as soon as the boats came within gunshot, but the shot from the vessels went over their heads. As soon as the men landed, the boats returned to the fleet, cutting off all means of retreat. No force could reach the summit in the face of such a fire of musketry, so the American troops were divided into three parties. One sought a practicable ascent at the right, one at the left, and the centre kept up a brisk fire to attract the attention of the enemy on the heights. Both the right and left parties gained the summit, followed by the centre, in the face of a galling fire, which they were powerless to return. Captain Warren's company of volunteers from Falmouth were the first to form on the heights, when all closed on the enemy, who, after a sharp skirmish, made their escape, leaving thirty men killed and wounded. Of the attacking party of four hundred, one hundred were killed or wounded. The engagement was short, but great pluck and courage were shown by the Americans. It has been said that no more brilliant exploit than this was accomplished by our forces during the war ; but this is the only bright spot in the record of the expedition. After the retreat of the enemy some slight intrenchments were thrown up by the sadly weakened little detachment, within seven hundred yards of the enemy's main works. These intrenchments were held by our men, and thus was made a good beginning.

The same morning a council of war was called of the land and naval officers. The former were for summoning the garrison to surrender, but the Commodore and the most of his officers were opposed to the measure. It was next proposed to storm the fort; but the Commodore refused to land any more of his marines, as those at the first landing suffered severely. The land force alone was deemed insufficient for a successful attack on the works, and a whaleboat express was despatched to Boston for a reinforcement. General Lovell now commenced a regular investment of works by zigzag trenches for Revere's insufficient cannon, and approached to musket-shot distance of the fort, so that not one of the garrison dared to show his head above the embankments.

It was afterwards ascertained that, if a surrender had been demanded when first proposed, the commanding general was prepared to capitulate, so imperfect were his defences. Commodore Saltonstall was self-willed, and disagreed with Generals Lovell and Wadsworth. During the two weeks delay the British strengthened their defences, and enclosed their works with chevaux-de-frise, with an abatis outside of all, which rendered the storming project impracticable if the expected reinforcement had arrived. The American Commodore kept up a daily cannonade with a show of an attempt to enter the harbor, but it was only a show. A deserter from the Americans informed the British commander of an intended attack the next day, which prevented any success.

On the 13th of August a lookout vessel brought General Lovell news that a British squadron of seven sail was entering Penobscot Bay, in answer to General McLane's application to Halifax on the first discovery of the American fleet. A retreat was immediately ordered by General Lovell, and conducted by General Wadsworth in the night, with so much skill that the whole of the troops were on board the transports undiscovered by the enemy. The British squadron entered the harbor the next morning, consisting of one seventy-four gunship, one frigate, and five smaller vessels, all under the command of Sir John Collier, with fifteen hundred troops on board. Saltonstall kept his position until the transports retreated up the river, when a general broadside from Collier's ship caused a disorderly flight, and a general chase and indiscriminate destruction of the American fleet. Several were blown up by their own crews, to prevent their falling into the hands of the enemy.

The troops and crews of the vessels left them

for the woods. Most of the officers and men of the fleet and army made their way through the woods guided by the Penobscot Indians, who were friendly to the Colonies through the war for independence. These struggling parties suffered every privation before reaching the settlements, subsisting on such game and fish as they were able to obtain. A large number were piloted by the Indians to Fort Halifax, where they were recruited and returned home by the Kennebec.

A court of inquiry as to the cause of the failure of the expedition gave as their opinion, " That the principal reason of the failure of the expedition was the want of the proper spirit on the part of the Commodore. That the destruction of the fleet was occasioned essentially because of his not exerting himself at all in the time of the retreat, by opposing the enemy's foremost ships in pursuit. . . . . That General Lovell, throughout the expedition and retreat, acted with proper courage and spirit; and had he been furnished with all the men ordered for the service, or been properly supported by the Commodore, he would probably have reduced the enemy." The court spoke in the highest terms of General Wadsworth. Upon this report the General Court adjudged " that Commodore Saltonstall be incompetent ever after to hold a commission in the service of the State, and that Generals Lovell and Wadsworth be honorably acquitted."

In answer to General Lovell's appeal for assistance by the whaleboat express to Boston, a regiment under Colonel Henry Jackson proceeded to Falmouth on their way to Penobscot, when they heard of the disaster to the expedition.

When I was a boy, sixty years ago, many of the men of Cumberland County who had been in the Bagaduce expedition were then living, — some of them were my own relatives. I have often heard angry discussions between those of the land and those of the naval service. The landsmen always assumed the aggressive, and had the best of the argument. It was the opinion of both, that, if General Wadsworth had been in chief command on shore, the gallant detachments which first gained the heights could not have been restrained until they had crossed bayonets with the garrison of the half-built fortress, and that was the time to have carried the works.

After the failure of the Bagaduce expedition the British pursued a system of outrageous plundering on the shores of Penobscot Bay and the neighboring coast, in which they were piloted and assisted by the numerous Tories who had gathered at Bagaduce and in the vicinity. To protect the people from this plundering, the Continental

Congress in 1780 ordered six hundred men to be detached from the three eastern brigades of the State, for eight months' service. Every soldier was ordered to march well equipped, within twenty-four hours after he was detached, or pay a fine of sixty pounds currency, which was to be applied to procure a substitute. The command of the whole Eastern department, between the Piscataqua and St. Croix, was given to General Wadsworth, with power to raise more troops if they were needed. He was also empowered to declare and execute martial law over territory ten miles in width, upon the coast eastward of Kennebec, according to the rules of the American army. His head-quarters were established at Thomaston. For the purpose of protecting his friends, the General found it necessary to draw a line of demarkation between them and their foes. He issued a proclamation prohibiting any intercourse with the enemy. This paper, of which I have a copy, is dated at Thomaston, 18th April, 1780, and declares the penalty of military execution for any infringement of it. The people of the islands east of Penobscot to Union River, "from their exposed situation," were ordered to hold themselves as neutrals. All persons joining the enemy were to be treated as deserters from the American army.

This proclamation did not have the desired effect. The most bitter of the Tories supposed that they would be protected by General McLane, but he disapproved of their plundering. Captain Mowatt of detestable memory, who was in command of the British squadron, was of a different character, and encouraged their depredations, when they became very aggressive. A stanch friend of the American cause at Broad Bay, named Soule, was shot in his bed, and his wife was wounded. This drew from General Wadsworth another proclamation, denouncing death to any one convicted of secreting or giving aid to the enemy. Soon after a man named Baum was detected in secreting and aiding Tories to reach Castine. He was tried by court-martial, found guilty of treason, and General Wadsworth ordered his execution by hanging the next morning, which was carried into effect. This effectually checked the intercourse with Bagaduce. A danghter of General Wadsworth, in writing of the circumstance to a son-in-law, in 1834, said, " My mother has told me that my father was greatly distressed at being obliged to execute the penalty of the law." General Wadsworth's wife was with him at the time.

After the term of service of the six hundred troops had expired, General Wadsworth was left with only six soldiers as a guard at his house, it being his intention also to leave within a week or two. His family consisted of his wife and son of five years, and Miss Fenno of Boston, a particular friend of Mrs. Wadsworth's.

Made acquainted with his defenceless condition by spies, General McLane, at Bagaduce, despatched a party of twenty-five men under Lieutenant Stockton to take him prisoner. They left their vessel four miles off and marched to his residence, arriving at about midnight, February 18, 1781. The General had plenty of fire-arms in his sleeping-room, and when his house was entered by the enemy he made a determined defence, until he was shot in the arm, when he surrendered, and was hurried off to the vessel. When he became weak from the loss of blood, he was set on a horse for the march. He suffered much from cold and pain from his wound. He was taken across the bay to Castine, and imprisoned in Fort George. He knew nothing for two weeks of the fate of his family, who had been exposed to the firing. At the request of General Wadsworth, General McLane sent a lieutenant with a boat's crew to Camden, across the bay, with letters to his family and to the Governor of the State, which were inspected previous to sealing. Finally, a letter was received from Mrs. Wadsworth containing an assurance that they were unharmed. General McLane treated his prisoner very politely, inviting him to eat at his own table, with guard of an orderly-sergeant, but refused him a parole or exchange. In the spring, four months after his seizure, Mrs. Wadsworth and Miss Fenno, with a passport from General McLane, arrived at Bagaduce, and were politely entertained at the fort for ten days. In the mean time orders had arrived from the commanding general at New York, in answer to a communication from General McLane. Their purport was learned from a hint conveyed to Miss Fenno by an officer, that the General was not to be exchanged, but would be sent to some English prison. When Miss Fenno left she gave the General all the information she dared to. She said, " General Wadsworth, take care of yourself." This the General interpreted to mean that he was to be conveyed to England, and he determined to make his escape from the fortress if possible. Soon after, a vessel arrived from Boston with a flag of truce from the Governor and Council, asking for an exchange for the General, and bringing a sum of money for his use, but the request was refused.

Major Barton, a resident of St. George's River, who had served the previous summer under General Wadsworth, was a prisoner in the same room with him. After a long preparation, and by obtaining a gimlet from the fort barber, they made their escape on the night of the 18th of June by passing through an opening previously and laboriously made in the board ceiling with the gimlet, the marks of which were filled with bread. They adroitly evaded the sentinels, but got separated in the darkness, both, however, getting off safely.

They kept much in the shoal water of the shores, to prevent being tracked by the bloodhounds which were kept at the fort for that purpose. The two friends came accidentally together on the next day. Major Barton dropped a glove in the darkness, which pointed out to their pursuers the route they had taken on leaving the fort. They however found a canoe, got across the river, and pursued their course through the woods by a pocket compass to the settlements, and were assisted to Thomaston, after much suffering. On arriving at his former residence, General Wadsworth found that his family had left for Boston, whither he followed them, after a brief stop at Falmouth, where he finally fixed his residence.

Here is a note from the General's daughter, mother of our poet : —

" Perhaps you would like to see my father's picture as it was when we came to this town after the war of the Revolution, in 1784.   Imagine to yourself a man of middle size, well-proportioned, with a military air, and who carried himself so truly that many thought him tall. His dress, a bright scarlet coat, buff small-clothes and vest, full ruffled bosom, ruffles over the hands, white stockings, shoes with silver buckles, white cravat bow in front, hair well powdered and tied behind in a club, so called. . . . . Of his character others may speak, but I cannot forbear to claim for him an uncommon share of benevolence and kind feeling.

" Z. W. L.

" January, 1848."

In 1797, President Dwight of Yale College, who had been a chaplain in the American army, visited Portland, and was the guest of General Wadsworth, from whom he says he " received an uninterrupted succession of civilities."   He also received from the General and wrote out a minute and thrilling account of his capture, imprisonment, and escape, which covers twenty-five printed pages.   General Wadsworth, at the time of its publication, vouched for its accuracy.[1]

The record of the births of his eleven children shows the places where the General lived at the time.   The oldest was born at Kingston, Mass.,

---

[1] See Dwight's Travels in New England.

in 1774, and died the next year at Dorchester. Charles Lee was born at Plymouth, January, 1776, and died at Hiram, Sept. 29, 1848. Zilpah was born at Duxbury, Jan. 6, 1778; died in Portland, March 12, 1851. Elizabeth, born in Boston, Sept. 21, 1779; died in Portland, Aug. 1, 1802. John, born at Plymouth, Sept. 1, 1781; graduated H. C. in 1800; died at Hiram, Jan. 22, 1860. Lucia, born at Plymouth, June 12, 1783; died in Portland, Oct. 17, 1864. Henry, born at Falmouth, Me., June 21, 1785; killed at Tripoli, Sept. 4, 1804. George, born in Portland, Jan. 6, 1788; died in Philadelphia, April 8, 1816. Alexander Scammell, born in Portland, May 7, 1790; died at Washington, April 5, 1851. Samuel Bartlett, born in Portland, Sept. 1, 1791; died at Eastport, Oct. 2, 1874. Peleg, born in Portland, Oct. 10, 1793; died at Hiram, Jan. 17, 1875.

The birth of a son in Plymouth, Sept. 7, 1781, shows that General Wadsworth took his family there on leaving his command in Maine. A daughter was also born there in 1783. It is known that he came to Falmouth in 1784. In December of that year he purchased of John Ingersoll of Boston, shipwright, for one hundred pounds lawful money, the lot of land in Falmouth on which he erected his buildings for a home. In the deed he is named of that town. The purchase is described as " lying northeast of a lot now possessed by Captain Arthur McLellan, being four rods in front, and running towards Back Cove, and containing one and one half acres." This is the Congress Street lot on which he erected his house and store.

Dr. Deane in his Diary says his store and barn were built in 1784. While he was building his house, he with his family lived in a building at the south corner of Franklin and Congress Streets, belonging to Captain Jonathan Paine. It was built for a barn, but probably had been occupied before as a dwelling, as it escaped Mowatt's burning ten years before, which compelled well-to-do people to occupy very humble quarters. This building was long afterwards finished for a dwelling-house by Elijah Adams, and burned in 1866. In the spring of 1785, General Wadsworth made preparation to erect his house. There had then been no attempt in the town to construct all the walls of a building of brick; indeed, there had been no suitable brick for walls made here. At that time brick buildings were expected to have a projecting base of several courses, the top one to be of brick fashioned for the purpose, the outer end of which formed a regular moulding when laid on edge and endwise, and the walls receded several inches to the perpendicular face. Several houses besides General Wadsworth's were commenced in this way. In the spring of 1785 the General obtained brick for his house in Philadelphia, including those for the base and a belt above the first story. John Nichols was the master mason.

Although the house was to be of only two stories, the walls were built sixteen inches thick, strong enough for a church tower. This required more bricks than had been expected, and at the close of the season the walls were not completed. There was no alternative but to secure the masonry from the weather, and wait for another spring. When that came more bricks were imported, and "the house that Jack (Nichols) built" was finished. It is yet standing, and shows good work in the artistic window-caps of brick. There was no other brick house built in town until three years after. The Wadsworth house, when originally finished, had a high pitched roof of two equal sides, and four chimneys. The store adjoined the house at the southeast, with an entrance door from the house, and was of two stories. Here the General sold all kinds of goods needed in the town and country trade. His name appears in the records, with some forty others, as licensed "retailers" of the town in 1785. What time he gave up the store is uncertain. The late

Edward Howe occupied it in 1805, who described it to me.

General Wadsworth was elected to the Massachusetts Senate in 1792, and the same year he was elected Representative to Congress, being the first from Cumberland District, and was successively elected to that office until 1806, when he declined a re-election. In 1798 the citizens of Portland gave him a public dinner, in approbation of his official conduct. Captain William Merrill related to me the circumstance, that when the seat of government was removed from Philadelphia to Washington, in 1801, General Wadsworth took passage in his vessel for Baltimore, that being the most speedy and comfortable way to reach Washington.

In 1790, General Wadsworth purchased from the State of Massachusetts 7,500 acres of wild land in the township which is now Hiram, on the Saco River. The price paid was twelve and a half cents per acre. He immediately commenced to clear a farm on a large scale, as is shown by a paragraph in the Eastern Herald of September 10, 1792, published in Portland. It says: " General Wadsworth thinks he has raised more than one thousand bushels of corn this season on burnt land, that is now out of danger of the frost, at a place called Great Ossipee, about thirty-six miles from this town. This is but the third year of his improvements." In 1790 the township contained a population of 186.

In 1795, General Wadsworth settled his son Charles Lee on his tract, and in 1800 he prepared to remove his own family there. In that year he began to build a large house on his land purchase, which is yet standing, one mile from Hiram village. The clay for the bricks of the chimneys was brought down Saco River three miles in a boat. This house was of two stories, with a railed outlook on the ridge between the two chimneys. There was a very large one-story kitchen adjoining, with an immense chimney and fireplace. Years after its building, the General's youngest son Peleg said that at the time of the erection of the house he was seven years old, and was left by his father to watch the fires in the eleven fireplaces, which were kindled to dry the new masonry, while he rode to the post-road for his mail, and that he had not felt such a weight of responsibility since.

The General took his family and household goods to his new home in the first of the winter, and commenced housekeeping in the new house, January 1, 1807. He, with his son Charles Lee, engaged in lumbering and farming. General Wadsworth was a skilful land surveyor and draftsman, and was much employed in the new township. He was chosen Selectman in 1812, and re-elected annually until 1818, and was twelve years Town Treasurer. He was a magistrate, and was looked upon as the patriarch of the town. He was a patron of education, and his home was the central point of the region for hospitality and culture. He was long a communicant of the Congregational Church, and so continued until his death in 1829, at the age of eighty-one. Mrs. Wadsworth died in 1825. Their graves are in a private enclosure on the home farm. The original modest headstones have given place to a more conspicuous monument of marble. The son Peleg, who was thirteen years old when the family moved to Hiram, spent the remainder of his life in that town, and died in 1875, at the age of eighty-one. It is a remarkable fact that General Wadsworth and his sons Charles Lee and Peleg, who all lived and died at Hiram, each reared eleven children. For the facts relating to General Wadsworth's life at Hiram I am indebted to his great-grandson, Llewellyn A. Wadsworth, who has in preparation a history of that town.

Two of the sons of General Wadsworth were officers in the United States navy. Henry became a lieutenant at the age of nineteen, and was attached to the schooner Scourge, in Commodore

Preble's squadron before Tripoli, in 1804. The last entry in his journal before the attack in which he lost his life was this: " We are in daily expectation of the Commodore's arrival from Syracuse with the gun-boats and bomb-vessels, and then, Tripoli, be on thy guard." The story of his sad death is told in the inscription on a marble cenotaph erected by his father to his memory, in the Eastern Cemetery in Portland, near the graves of the captains of the Enterprise and Boxer.

It is from this gallant officer, his uncle, that the poet Longellow received his baptismal name.

The General's ninth child was Alexander Scammell Wadsworth, born in Portland in 1790. When the Constitution frigate fought her memorable battle, in August, 1812, in which she captured the British frigate Guerriere, after having her three masts shot away by the Americans, Alexander Wadsworth was second lieutenant of the victorious ship. The first lieutenant, Morris, was severely wounded early in the action, when Lieutenant Wadsworth of course took his place, then only twenty-four. So well did he acquit himself that his fellow-townsmen of Portland presented him with a sword for his gallantry. Lieutenant Wadsworth was an officer on board the ship which conveyed our Minister, Joel Barlow, to France in 1811, and was presented with

[*S. W. Face.*]

In Memory of

HENRY WADSWORTH,

SON OF

PELEG WADSWORTH,

LIEUT. U. S. NAVY,

WHO FELL

BEFORE THE WALLS OF TRIPOLI

ON THE EVE OF 4th SEPT.

1804

IN THE 20th YEAR OF HIS AGE

BY THE EXPLOSION OF A
FIRE SHIP
WHICH HE WITH OTHERS
GALLANTLY CONDUCTED
AGAINST THE ENEMY.

[*S. E. Face.*]

DETERMINED

AT ONCE THEY PREFER DEATH

AND THE

DESTRUCTION OF THE ENEMY

TO CAPTIVITY

AND

TORTURING SLAVERY.

Com. Preble's Letter.

[*N. E. Face.*]

MY COUNTRY CALLS
THIS WORLD ADIEU
I HAVE ONE LIFE
THAT LIFE I GIVE FOR YOU

———

Capt. RICHARD SOMERS.

———

Lieut. HENRY WADSWORTH.

———

Lieut. JOSEPH ISRAEL.

———

AND 10 BRAVE SEAMEN
VOLUNTEERS
WERE THE DEVOTED
BAND.

[*N. W. Face.*]

AN HONOR TO HIS
COUNTRY
AND AN EXAMPLE TO
ALL EXCELLENT
YOUTH.

Resolve of Congress.

MARBLE CENOTAPH IN PORTLAND CEMETERY, ERECTED TO
LIEUT. HENRY WADSWORTH.

a sword by that gentleman. The Lieutenant rose to the rank of Commodore, and died in Washington in 1851, aged sixty-one.

Another of the children of General Wadsworth, Zilpah, performed her part in life as bravely, and died as much beloved and honored, as did her gallant brothers of the navy. She was born in Duxbury, January 6, 1778, while her father was in the army. When the family first occupied the brick house in Portland, she was eight years old, and recollected the inconveniences and discomforts of the unfinished quarters in which they lived while the house was building.

In 1799, June 25, Zilpah Wadsworth, in behalf of the ladies of Portland, presented a military standard to a volunteer company called the Federal volunteers. It was the first uniformed company in Maine. Joseph C. Boyd was captain, and the ensign who received the standard and replied to the presentation address was named Wiggin. In after years Mrs. Longfellow described to her daughters the rehearsal of her speech, and the waving of the banner on the back steps of her father's house to her sister, who personated Ensign Wiggin. The presentation was from the front portico of that historic mansion. The street has been filled up since then, hiding the stone steps. The motto on the flag was, " Defend the Laws." On one side were painted the arms of the United States, and on the other the same, united with the arms of Massachusetts.

In 1804, Zilpah Wadsworth became the wife of Stephen Longfellow, and first kept house in a two-story wooden building, yet standing on the south corner of Congress and Temple Streets. When her father's family left the brick house for a new home in the country, in 1807, she, with a family of a husband and two sons, took the old homestead. Mr. Longfellow moved the store, and in its place built the brick vestibule at the east corner, over which he placed a modest sign which was there within my knowledge; it read, "Stephen Longfellow, Counsellor at Law." He occupied the eastern front room for his law office, opening from the brick entry. In this office, several young students read Coke and Blackstone, who became prominent lawyers of Cumberland County.

One day in 1814 or 1815, while Mrs. Longfellow was indisposed, and the family physician was in attendance, the servant overheated the kitchen flue, which took fire and communicated it to the attic, of which the family knew nothing until it broke out through the roof. Mr. Longfellow was the chief fire-ward of the department; but his first thought was of his sick wife, whom he hastily inquired for of Dr. Weed. He told Mr. Long-fellow to look to the fire, and he would take care of his wife. When it became evident that the house must be flooded, the Doctor, who was a tall, muscular man, wrapped Mrs. Longfellow in a blanket and carried her in his arms into Madam Preble's, the next door, now the hotel. A lady of the family, who was then a child, described the scene to me. Her first realization of the danger was from seeing her father standing on a post of the front fence, with a brass trumpet to his mouth, giving loud orders to the gathering firemen, and gesticulating violently. After it had nearly de-stroyed the roof, the fire was extinguished.

To increase the accommodations for his large family, Mr. Longfellow added to the house a third story, and a low four-sided or "hipped" roof took the place of the high two-sided one, with the chimneys the same. And thus repaired, the venerable structure, around which so much of his-torical interest clusters, has remained to the pres-ent time. Although overshadowed and crowded upon by its more pretentious neighbors, it is more inquired for now by strangers than any other house in the city. May the polite and refined descendant of its builder, who is now its mistress, long continue to preside there and dispense its traditional hospitalities!

No. II.

GENEALOGIES.

GENEALOGY OF GENERAL PELEG WADSWORTH.

I.

THE ancestor of the name in the Old Colony was

CHRISTOPHER WADSWORTH, or, as it was early abridged, Xtofer Waddesworth, from Yorkshire, Eng., where there is a town of the same name. He was one of the earliest settlers of Duxbury, Mass.

In 1633, he was chosen 1st Constable of the town, then an office of trust and responsibility.

1640.   He was chosen Deputy, or Representative.

1666.   Selectman, — several times re-elected.

1680.   He died probably.

1677.   July 31, his will is dated.   Est. £70 3 4.   His wife was Grace.

II.

1638.   His 2d son John^2 [3–2] was born.

1667.   John^2 m. Abigail Andrews, daughter of Joseph. July 25.   She was b. 1647, and d. 1723; he d. 1700, May 15th; was a Deacon of the Church in Duxbury.

III.

His son John[3] [14–3] b. 1671, Mar. 12.

1704. M. Mercy Wiswell, June 25.

1718. M. 2d wife, Widow Mary Verdie of Boston ; had six children, all by first wife except Mary, the youngest, b. 1721.

1750. He died, May 3, aged 78 years.

IV.

1715. His son Peleg [41–5] was born, Aug. 29.

1740. M. Susanna Sampson ; was a Deacon.

V.

1748. His son General Peleg [82–5] was b. May 6, at Duxbury ; taught school at Plymouth.

1765. He entered Harvard College.

1769. Graduated Harvard College.

1772. June 18th, m. Elizabeth Bartlett, who was born Aug. 9, 1753, at Plymouth, and d. 1825, July 20th, at Hiram, Me. She was daughter of Samuel Bartlett, Esq., by his second wife, Elizabeth Lothrop Witherell, and great-great-granddaughter of the 1st Robert Bartlett, who was b. in Eng. in 1603. Peleg [82–5] had 11 children, 8 sons and 3 daughters, and d. at Hiram, Me., 1829, Sept. 29, æt. 81 years.

1775. He joined the Continental army at Roxbury. Captain of a company of minute-men.

1776. Commissioned by Congress as Captain, and employed by Gen. Thomas as Engineer in laying out the lines of defence in Roxbury and Dorchester, and was Aid to Maj.-Gen. Ward when the Heights were occupied.

1778. Appointed Adj.-Gen. Mass. Militia.

1779. Was second in command under Gen. Lovell on Penobscot expedition.

1781. Was attacked, shot, and captured at So. Thomaston in February, carried to Castine, and imprisoned by the British in Fort George, whence he made his remarkable escape in June. (See Dwight, Journal, etc.)

1784. Established himself in Portland, Me., and built the first brick house erected there, 1784–85.

1792. Chosen Senator to Massachusetts Legislature.

1792. Chosen first Representative to the U. S. Congress at Philadelphia, and served 14 years.

1798. Received a public dinner from citizens.

1806. Declined a re-election to Congress, and retired to private life.

1807. Moved to Hiram, Oxford Co., Maine, and improved one third of the township, which was granted to him for his military services by the Legislature. It was called on the map Hiram, or Wadsworth Grant.

1829. Died at Hiram, Me.

DESCENT OF LONGFELLOW FROM JOHN ALDEN.

His mother, Zilpah Wadsworth, was daughter of General Peleg Wadsworth, who was son of Deacon Peleg W. of Duxbury, born 1715, died ——, and of Susanna Sampson, born 1720, married 1740. Susanna was daughter of John Sampson, who was born 1688, and was married, 1718, to Priscilla Bartlett, born 1697, died 1758. John Sampson was son of Stephen S., born about 1650, and of Priscilla Paybodie, born 1653. Priscilla was daughter of William Pabodie, who was born 1620, married 1644, and died 1707, and of Elizabeth Alden, born 1625, died 1717. Elizabeth was daughter of John Alden and Priscilla Mullen, who came in the Mayflower.

ANOTHER LINE OF DESCENT.

Ruth Pabodie, daughter of William Pabodie and Elizabeth Alden, was married in 1672 to Benjamin Bartlett; and their daughter Priscilla, having married John Sampson in 1718, was the mother of Susanna Sampson, the mother of General Peleg Wadsworth.

No. III.

[From the New York Tribune, April 2, 1882.]

LONGFELLOW.

BY WILLIAM WINTER.

ALONE, at night, he heard them sigh,
  These wild March winds that beat his tomb ;
Alone, at night, from those that die
  He sought one ray to light his gloom.

And still he heard the night-winds moan,
  And still the mystery closed him round,
And still the darkness, cold and lone,
  Sent forth no ray, returned no sound.

But Time at last the answer brings,
  And he, past all our suns and snows,
At rest with peasants and with kings,
  Like them the wondrous secret knows.

Alone, at night, we hear them sigh,
  These wild March winds that stir his pall ;
And, helpless, wandering. lost, we cry
  To his dim ghost to tell us all.

He loved us, while he lingered here ;
  We loved him, — never love more true !
He will not leave, in doubt and fear,
  The human grief that once he knew.

For never yet was born the day,
   When, faint of heart and weak of limb,
One suffering creature turned away,
   Unhelped, unsoothed, uncheered by him !

But still through darkness dense and bleak
   The winds of March moan wildly round.
And still we feel that all we seek
   Ends in that sigh of vacant sound.

He cannot tell us — none can tell —
   What waits behind the mystic veil !
Yet he who lived and died so well,
   In that, perchance, has told the tale.

Not to the wastes of Nature drift —
   Else were this world an evil dream —
The crown and soul of Nature's gift,
   By Avon or by Charles's stream.

His heart was pure, his purpose high,
   His thought serene, his patience vast;
He put all strifes of passion by,
   And lived to God, from first to last.

His song was like the pine-tree's sigh
   At midnight o'er a poet's grave,
Or like the sea-bird's distant cry,
   Borne far across the twilight wave.

There is no flower of meek delight,
   There is no star of heavenly pride,
That shines not sweeter and more bright
   Because he lived, loved, sang, and died.

Wild winds of March, his requiem sing !
  Weep o'er him, April's sorrowing skies !
Till come the tender flowers of Spring
  To deck the pillow where he lies ; —

Till violets pour their purple flood,
  That wandering myrtle shall not lack,
And, royal with the summer's blood,
  The roses that he loved come back ;

Till all that Nature gives of light,
  To rift the gloom and point the way,
Shall sweetly pierce our mortal night,
  And symbol his immortal day !

No. IV.

CORRESPONDENCE WITH CHARLES LANMAN.[1]

[From the New York Tribune, April 13, 1882.]

THE WRECK OF THE HESPERUS ; NORMAN'S WOE ; LONG-FELLOW, SUMNER, AND WHITTIER, WITH MAJOR BEN PERLEY POORE, AT INDIAN HILL.

IN 1871, while exhibiting a portfolio of my sketches in oil for a nephew of Mr. Longfellow, we stumbled upon a view of Norman's Woe, near Cape Ann, when he remarked, "My uncle should see that picture, for I know it would greatly interest him." On the next day, accordingly, I packed up the picture, and, with another, — a view on the coast of Nova Scotia, the home of Evangeline, — sent it off by express to Mr. Long-

[1] Mr. Lanman is at once an artist and an author, and is widely known from his works. The genial Irving called him "the picturesque explorer of America." He was formerly the private secretary of Daniel Webster, afterwards a librarian in Washington, and has now for the past ten years been the American Secretary of the Japanese Legation. He announces for publication a volume entitled "Haphazard Personalities."

fellow, accompanied by a note of explanation, in which I recalled the fact of our meeting many years before at the house of Park Benjamin, in New York, who was the first to publish the poem about the Hesperus, and who paid for it the pittance of twenty-five dollars. The letter which Mr. Longfellow sent me in return, worth more than a thousand sketches, was as follows: —

Cambridge, November 24, 1871.

My dear Sir, — Last night I had the pleasure of receiving your friendly letter and the beautiful pictures that came with it; and I thank you cordially for the welcome gift and the kind remembrance that prompted it. They are both very interesting to me; particularly the reef of Norman's Woe. What you say of the ballad is also very gratifying, and induces me to send you in return a bit of autobiography.

Looking over a journal for 1839, a few days ago, I found the following entries : —

" *December* 17. — News of shipwrecks, horrible, on the coast. Forty bodies washed ashore near Gloucester. One woman lashed to a piece of wreck. There is a reef called Norman's Woe, where many of these took place. Among others the schooner Hesperus. Also, the Seaflower, on Black Rock. I will write a ballad on this.

" *December* 30. — Wrote last evening a notice of Allston's Poems, after which sat till one o'clock by the fire, smoking ; when suddenly it came into my mind to write the ballad of the schooner Hesperus, which I accordingly did. Then went to bed, but could not sleep. New thoughts were running in my mind, and I got up to add them to the ballad. It was three by the clock."

All this is of no importance but to myself. However, I like sometimes to recall the circumstances under which a poem was written ; and as you express a liking for this one, it may perhaps interest you to know why and when and how it came into existence. I had quite forgotten about its first publication ; but I find a letter from Park Benjamin, dated January 7, 1840, beginning (you will recognize his style) as follows :—

" Your ballad, 'The Wreck of the Hesperus,' is grand. Enclosed are twenty-five dollars (the sum you mentioned) for it, paid by the proprietors of 'The New World,' in which glorious paper it will resplendently coruscate on Saturday next."

Pardon this gossip, and believe me, with renewed thanks, yours faithfully,

HENRY W. LONGFELLOW.

During the summer of 1873, while spending a few weeks at Indian Hill, in Massachusetts, the delightful residence of Ben Perley Poore, it was again my privilege to meet Mr. Longfellow. He had come down from Nahant with his friend, Charles Sumner, for the purpose of visiting, for the first time, the Longfellow homestead in Newbury. After that visit he came by invitation, with the Senator, to Indian Hill, where they enjoyed an early dinner and a bit of old wine, after which Mr. Poore took us all in his carriage on a visit to the poet John G. Whittier, at Amesbury. The day was charming, the route we followed was down the Merrimack, and very lovely, and the conversation of the lions was of course delightful. We found Mr. Whittier at home, and it was not only a great treat to see him there, but a noted event to meet socially and under one roof three such men as Whittier, Sumner, and Longfellow. The deportment of the two poets was, to me, most captivating. The host, in his simple dress, was as shy as a schoolboy, while Mr. Longfellow, with his white and flowing hair, and jolly laughter, reminded me of one of his own Vikings; and when Mr. Whittier brought out and exhibited to us an antislavery document which he had signed forty years before, I could not help recalling some of the splendid things which that trio of great men had written on the subject of slavery. The drive to Newburyport, whence Mr. Sumner and Mr. Longfellow were to return to Nahant, was not less delightful than had been the preceding one; and the kindly words which were spoken of Mr. Whittier proved that he was highly honored and loved by his noted friends, as he is by the world at large. Before parting from Mr. Longfellow he took me one side and spoke with great interest of the old homestead he had that morning visited, and expressed a wish that I should make a sketch of it for him, as it was then two hundred years old, and rapidly going to decay. On the following morning I went to the spot and complied with his request; a few weeks afterward I sent him a finished picture of the house, not forgetting the well-sweep and the old stone horse-block, in which he felt a special interest; and he acknowledged the receipt of the picture in these words : —

CAMBRIDGE, October 18, 1873.

MY DEAR SIR, — I have had the pleasure of receiving your very friendly note, and the picture of the old homestead at Newbury, for both of which I pray you to accept my most cordial thanks. Be assured that I value your gift highly, and appreciate the kindness which prompted it, and the trouble you took in making the portraits of the old house and tree. They are very exact, and will always remind me of that pleasant summer day and Mr. Poore's chateau and his charming family, and yours. If things could ever be done twice over in this world, which they cannot, I should like to live that day over again.

With kind regards to Mrs. Lanman, not forgetting a word and a kiss to your little Japanese ward (Ume Tsuda), I am, my dear sir, yours truly,

HENRY W. LONGFELLOW.

No. V.

[From "The Independent," April 6, 1882.]

MR. LONGFELLOW'S EARLY POEMS.

HITHERTO OMITTED FROM ALL AMERICAN COLLECTIONS.

OF Mr. Longfellow's juvenile poems, published mostly in a forgotten magazine, he recovered only seven, which he allowed to remain in his collections under the title of " Earlier Poems." They have, however, been collected in England by Richard Herne Shepherd, and published by Pickering & Co. From that volume we reprint them, omitting those which are made familiar by Longfellow's own preservation of them. Mr. Shepherd says in his Preface : —

" Seventeen out of the twenty-one poems that compose this little volume appeared during the years 1824–26 in a brief-lived fortnightly Transatlantic magazine, entitled 'The United States Literary Gazette.' The author had not completed his eighteenth year when the first of them appeared, and had only just passed his nineteenth when the last was published. An exact account of the dates of their appearance will not be without interest.

"Poems by H. W. Longfellow in the United States Literary Gazette.

I.

Thanksgiving. 'When first in ancient time from Jubal's tongue.' Nov. 15, 1824.

II.

Autumnal Nightfall. 'Round Autumn's mouldering urn.' Dec. 1, 1824.

III.

Italian Scenery. 'Night rests in beauty on Mont Alto.' Dec. 15, 1824.

IV.

The Lunatic Girl. 'Most beautiful, most gentle!' Jan. 1, 1825.

V.

The Venetian Gondolier. 'Here rest the weary oar!' Jan. 15, 1825.

VI.

Woods in Winter. 'When winter winds are piercing chill.' (Partly reprinted in the Earlier Poems.) Feb. 1, 1825.

VII.

Dirge over a Nameless Grave. 'By yon still river, where the wave.' March 14, 1825.

VIII.

A Song of Savoy. 'As the dim twilight shrouds.' March 15, 1825.

IX.

An April Day (reprinted). April 15, 1825.

X.

The Indian Hunter. 'When the summer harvest was gathered in.' May 15, 1825.

XI.

Hymn of the Moravian Nuns (reprinted). June 1, 1825.

XII.

Sunrise on the Hills (reprinted). July 1, 1825.

XIII.

Jeckoyva. 'They made the warrior's grave beside.' Aug. 1, 1825.

XIV.

The Sea Diver. 'My way is on the bright blue sea.' Aug. 15, 1825.

XV.

Autumn. 'With what a glory' (reprinted). Oct. 1, 1825.

XVI.

Musings. 'I sat by my window one night.' Nov. 15, 1825.

XVII.

Song. 'Where from the eye of day.' April 1, 1826.

"And here the contributions dropped, nor did the magazine itself (which contained also contributions from other men who have since risen to celebrity) long survive.

"The curious part of the affair is that Longfellow, when issuing his first collected volume of poems, thirteen years later ('Voices of the Night,' Boston, 1839), thought it worth while to include five (by no means the best) of these early pieces, but did not care to rescue the other twelve (not only the larger, but by far the better portion of these *juvenilia*) from their *oubliette*.

"'Most of Mr. Longfellow's poetry,' writes George Cheever, in 1831, 'indeed, we believe nearly all that has been published, appeared, during his college life, in the United States Literary Gazette. It displays a very refined taste and a very pure vein of poetical feeling. It possesses what has been a rare quality in the American poets,—simplicity of expression, without any attempt to startle the reader, or to produce an effect by far-sought epithets. There is much sweetness in his imagery and language ; and sometimes he is hardly excelled by any one for the quiet accuracy exhibited in his pictures of natural objects. His poetry will not easily be forgotten.'[1]

"To such praise we need add little ; nor is it our intention to enter into detailed criticism of these slight first-fruits of Longfellow's muse. If the savor of them

---

[1] "The American Commonplace Book of Poetry, with Occasional Notes." By George B. Cheever. Boston, 1831.

is sweet, the reader will not be ungrateful to us for cull-
ing them from the tangled wilderness where they lay un-
heeded and in danger of perishing."

THANKSGIVING.

WHEN first in ancient time from Jubal's tongue
The tuneful anthem filled the morning air,
To sacred hymnings and elysian song
His music-breathing shell the minstrel woke.
Devotion breathed aloud from every chord :
The voice of praise was heard in every tone,
And prayer, and thanks to Him the Eternal One,
To Him, that with bright inspiration touched
The high and gifted lyre of heavenly song,
And warmed the soul with new vitality.
A stirring energy through Nature breathed :
The voice of adoration from her broke,
Swelling aloud in every breeze, and heard
Long in the sullen waterfall, — what time
Soft Spring or hoary Autumn threw on earth
Its bloom or blighting, — when the Summer smiled,
Or Winter o'er the year's sepulchre mourned.
The Deity was there ! — a nameless spirit
Moved in the breasts of men to do Him homage ;
And when the morning smiled, or evening pale
Hung weeping o'er the melancholy urn,
They came beneath the broad o'erarching trees,
And in their tremulous shadow worshipped oft,
Where pale the vine clung round their simple altars,
And gray moss mantling hung. Above was heard
The melody of winds, breathed out as the green trees
Bowed to their quivering touch in living beauty,

And birds sang forth their cheerful hymns.   Below
The bright and widely wandering rivulet
Struggled and gushed amongst the tangled roots
That choked its reedy-fountain, and dark rocks
Worn smooth by the constant current.   Even there
The listless wave, that stole with mellow voice
Where reeds grew rank on the rushy-fringed brink,
And the green sedge bent to the wandering wind,
Sang with a cheerful song of sweet tranquillity.
Men felt the heavenly influence, and it stole
Like balm into their hearts, till all was peace ;
And even the air they breathed, the light they saw,
Became religion ; for the ethereal spirit
That to soft music wakes the chords of feeling,
And mellows everything to beauty, moved
With cheering energy within their breasts,
And made all holy there, — for all was love.
The morning stars, that sweetly sang together,
The moon, that hung at night in the mid-sky,
Dayspring, and eventide, and all the fair
And beautiful forms of nature, had a voice
Of eloquent worship.   Ocean with its tides
Swelling and deep, where low the infant storm
Hung on his dun, dark cloud, and heavily beat
The pulses of the sea, sent forth a voice
Of awful adoration to the spirit
That, wrapt in darkness, moved upon its face.
And when the bow of evening arched the east,
Or, in the moonlight pale, the curling wave
Kissed with a sweet embrace the sea-worn beach,
And soft the song of winds came o'er the waters,
The mingled melody of wind and wave
Touched like a heavenly anthem on the ear ;

For it arose a tuneful hymn of worship.
And have *our* hearts grown cold ?   Are there on earth
No pure reflections caught from heavenly light ?
Have our mute lips no hymn, — our souls no song ?
Let him that in the summer day of youth
Keeps pure the holy fount of youthful feeling,
And him that in the nightfall of his years
Lies down in his last sleep, and shuts in peace
His dim pale eyes on life's short wayfaring,
Praise him that rules the destiny of man.
Sunday Evening, October, 1824.

AUTUMNAL NIGHTFALL.

ROUND Autumn's mouldering urn
Loud mourns the chill and cheerless gale,
When nightfall shades the quiet vale,
And stars in beauty burn.

'T is the year's eventide.
The wind, like one that sighs in pain
O'er joys that ne'er will bloom again,
Mourns on the far hillside.

And yet my pensive eye
Rests on the faint blue mountain long,
And for the fairy-land of song,
That lies beyond, I sigh.

The moon unveils her brow ;
In the mid-sky her urn glows bright,
And in her sad and mellowing light
The valley sleeps below.

Upon the hazel gray
The lyre of Autumn hangs unstrung,
And o'er its tremulous chords are flung
The fringes of decay.

I stand deep musing here,
Beneath the dark and motionless beech,
Whilst wandering winds of nightfall reach
My melancholy ear.

The air breathes chill and free ;
A Spirit in soft music calls
From Autumn's gray and moss-grown halls,
And round her withered tree.

The hoar and mantled oak,
With moss and twisted ivy brown,
Bends in its lifeless beauty down
Where weeds the fountain choke.

That fountain's hollow voice
Echoes the sound of precious things ;
Of early feeling's tuneful springs
Choked with our blighted joys.

Leaves, that the night-wind bears
To earth's cold bosom with a sigh,
Are types of our mortality,
And of our fading years.

The tree that shades the plain,
Wasting and hoar as time decays,
Spring shall renew with cheerful days, —
But not my joys again.

ITALIAN SCENERY.

Night rests in beauty on Mont Alto.
Beneath its shade the beauteous Arno sleeps
In Vallombrosa's bosom, and dark trees
Bend with a calm and quiet shadow down
Upon the beauty of that silent river.
Still in the west a melancholy smile
Mantles the lips of day, and twilight pale
Moves like a spectre in the dusky sky ;
While eve's sweet star on the fast fading year
Smiles calmly.   Music steals at intervals
Across the water, with a tremulous swell,
From out the upland dingle of tall firs,
And a faint footfall sounds where dim and dark
Hangs the gray willow from the river's brink,
O'ershadowing its current.   Slowly there
The lover's gondola drops down the stream,
Silent, save when its dipping oar is heard,
Or in its eddy sighs the rippling wave.
Mouldering and moss-grown, through the lapse of years,
In motionless beauty stands the giant oak,
Whilst those that saw its green and flourishing youth
Are gone and are forgotten.   Soft the fount,
Whose secret springs the star-light pale discloses,
Gushes in hollow music, and beyond
The broader river sweeps its silent way,
Mingling a silver current with that sea,
Whose waters have no tides, coming nor going.
On noiseless wing along that fair blue sea
The halcyon flits, and where the wearied storm
Left a loud moaning, all is peace again.

A calm is on the deep!   The winds that came
O'er the dark sea-surge with a tremulous breathing,
And mourned on the dark cliff where weeds grew rank
And to the autumnal death-dirge the deep sea
Heaved its long billows, with a cheerless song
Have passed away to the cold earth again,
Like a wayfaring mourner.   Silently
Up from the calm sea's dim and distant verge,
Full and unveiled the moon's broad disk emerges.
On Tivoli, and where the fairy hues
Of autumn glow upon Abruzzi's woods,
The silver light is spreading.   Far above,
Encompassed with their thin, cold atmosphere,
The Apennines uplift their snowy brows,
Glowing with colder beauty, where unheard
The eagle screams in the fathomless ether,
And stays his wearied wing.   Here let us pause!
The spirit of these solitudes — the soul
That dwells within these steep and difficult places —
Speaks a mysterious language to mine own,
And brings unutterable musings.   Earth
Sleeps in the shades of nightfall, and the sea
Spreads like a thin blue haze beneath my feet,
Whilst the gray columns and the mouldering tombs
Of the Imperial City, hidden deep
Beneath the mantle of their shadows, rest.
My spirit looks on earth !   A heavenly voice
Comes silently : " Dreamer, is earth thy dwelling ?
Lo ! nursed within that fair and fruitful bosom
Which has sustained thy being, and within
The colder breast of Ocean, lie the germs
Of thine own dissolution !   E'en the air,
That fans the clear blue sky, and gives thee strength,

Up from the sullen lake of mouldering reeds,
And the wide waste of forest, where the osier
Thrives in the damp and motionless atmosphere,
Shall bring the dire and wasting pestilence
And blight thy cheek.   Dream thou of higher things ;
This world is not thy home !"   And yet my eye
Rests upon earth again !   How beautiful,
Where wild Velino heaves its sullen waves
Down the high cliff of gray and shapeless granite,
Hung on the curling mist, the moonlight bow
Arches the perilous river !   A soft light
Silvers the Albanian mountains, and the haze
That rests upon their summits mellows down
The austerer features of their beauty.   Faint
And dim-discovered glow the Sabine hills,
And, listening to the sea's monotonous shell,
High on the cliffs of Terracina stands
The castle of the royal Goth [1] in ruins.

But night is in her wane : day's early flush
Glows like a hectic on her fading cheek,
Wasting its beauty.   And the opening dawn
With cheerful lustre lights the royal city,
Where with its proud tiara of dark towers
It sleeps upon its own romantic bay.

THE LUNATIC GIRL.

Most beautiful, most gentle !   Yet how lost
To all that gladdens the fair earth ; the eye
That watched her being ; the maternal care

[1] Theodoric.

That kept and nourished her ; and the calm light
That steals from our own thoughts, and softly rests
On youth's green valleys and smooth-sliding waters !
Alas ! few suns of life, and fewer winds,
Had withered or had wasted the fresh rose
That bloomed upon her cheek ; but one chill frost
Came in that early Autumn, when ripe thought
Is rich and beautiful, and blighted it ;
And the fair stalk grew languid day by day,
And drooped, and drooped, and shed its many leaves.
'T is said that some have died of love, and some,
That once from beauty's high romance had caught
Love's passionate feelings and heart-wasting cares,
Have spurned life's threshold with a desperate foot:
And others have gone mad, — and she was one !
Her lover died at sea ; and they had felt
A coldness for each other when they parted ;
But love returned again, and to her ear
Came tidings that the ship which bore her lover .
Had suddenly gone down at sea, and all were lost.
I saw her in her native vale, when high
The aspiring lark up from the reedy river
Mounted on cheerful pinion ; and she sat
Casting smooth pebbles into a clear fountain,
And marking how they sunk ; and oft she sighed
For him that perished thus in the vast deep.
She had a sea-shell, that her lover brought
From the far-distant ocean, and she pressed
Its smooth cold lips unto her ear, and thought
It whispered tidings of the dark blue sea ;
And sad she cried, " The tides are out ! — and now
I see his corse upon the stormy beach ! "
Around her neck a string of rose-lipped shells,

And coral, and white pearl, was loosely hung,
And close beside her lay a delicate fan,
Made of the halcyon's blue wing ; and when
She looked upon it, it would calm her thoughts
As that bird calms the ocean, — for it gave
Mournful, yet pleasant memory.   Once I marked,
When through the mountain hollows and green woods
That bent beneath its footsteps the loud wind
Came with a voice as of the restless deep,
She raised her head, and on her pale cold cheek
A beauty of diviner seeming came :
And then she spread her hands, and smiled, as if
She welcomed a long-absent friend, — and then
Shrunk timorously back again, and wept.
I turned away : a multitude of thoughts,
Mournful and dark, were crowding on my mind,
And as I left that lost and ruined one, —
A living monument that still on earth
There is warm love and deep sincerity, —
She gazed upon the west, where the blue sky
Held, like an ocean, in its wide embrace
Those fairy islands of bright cloud, that lay
So calm and quietly in the thin ether.
And then she pointed where, alone and high,
One little cloud sailed onward, like a lost
And wandering bark, and fainter grew, and fainter,
And soon was swallowed up in the blue depths.
And when it sunk away, she turned again
With sad despondency and tears to earth.

Three long and weary months, — yet not a whisper
Of stern reproach for that cold parting !   Then
She sat no longer by her favorite fountain !
She was at rest forever.

THE VENETIAN GONDOLIER.

HERE rest the weary oar ! — soft airs
　Breathe out in the o'erarching sky ;
And Night — sweet Night — serenely wears
　A smile of peace ; her noon is nigh.

Where the tall fir in quiet stands,
　And waves, embracing the chaste shores,
Move o'er sea-shells and bright sands,
　Is heard the sound of dipping oars.

Swift o'er the wave the light bark springs,
　Love's midnight hour draws lingering near :
And list ! — his tuneful viol strings
　The young Venetian Gondolier.

Lo ! on the silver-mirrored deep,
　On earth and her embosomed lakes,
And where the silent rivers sweep,
　From the thin cloud fair moonlight breaks.

Soft music breathes around, and dies
　On the calm bosom of the sea ;
Whilst in her cell the novice sighs
　Her vespers to her rosary.

At their dim altars bow fair forms,
　In tender charity for those
That, helpless left to life's rude storms,
　Have never found this calm repose.

The bell swings to its midnight chime,
　Relieved against the deep blue sky !
Haste ! — dip the oar again ! — 't is time
　To seek Genevra's balcony.

DIRGE OVER A NAMELESS GRAVE.

By yon still river, where the wave
  Is winding slow at evening's close,
The beech, upon a.nameless grave,
  Its sadly-moving shadow throws.

O'er the fair woods the.sun looks down
  Upon the many twinkling leaves,
And twilight's mellow shades are brown,
  Where darkly the green turf upheaves.

The river glides in silence there,
  And hardly waves the sapling tree :
Sweet flowers are springing, and the air
  Is full of balm, — but where is she !

They bade her wed a son of pride,
  And leave the hopes she cherished long ;
She loved but one, — and would not hide
  A love which knew no wrong.

And months went sadly on, and years ;
  And she was wasting day by day :
At length she died ; and many tears
  Were shed, that she should pass away.

Then came a gray old man, and knelt
  With bitter weeping by her tomb ;
And others mourned for him, who felt
  That he had sealed a daughter's doom.

The funeral train has long past on,
  And time wiped dry the father's tear !
Farewell, lost maiden ! there is one
  That mourns thee yet,— and he is here.

A SONG OF SAVOY.

As the dim twilight shrouds
  The mountain's purple crest,
And Summer's white and folded clouds
  Are glowing in the west,
Loud shouts come up the rocky dell,
And voices hail the' evening bell.

Faint is the goatherd's song,
  And sighing comes the breeze :
The silent river sweeps along
  Amid its bending trees,
And the full moon shines faintly there,
And music fills the evening air.

Beneath the waving firs
  The tinkling cymbals sound ;
And as the wind the foliage stirs,
  I feel the dancers bound
Where the green branches, arched above,
Bend over this fair scene of love.

And he is there, that sought
  My young heart long ago !
But he has left me, — though I thought
  He ne'er could leave me so.
Ah ! lovers' vows, — how frail are they !
And his — were made but yesterday.

Why comes he not ? I call
  In tears upon him yet ;
'T were better ne'er to love at all,
  Than love, and then forget !

Why comes he not ?   Alas! I should
Reclaim him still, if weeping could.

But see, — he leaves the glade,
   And beckons me away:
He comes to seek his mountain maid;
   I cannot chide his stay.
Glad sounds along the valley swell,
And voices hail the evening bell.

THE INDIAN HUNTER.

WHEN the summer harvest was gathered in,
And the sheaf of the gleaner grew white and thin,
And the ploughshare was in its furrow left,
Where the stubble land had been lately cleft,
An Indian hunter, with unstrung bow,
Looked down where the valley lay stretched below.

He was a stranger there, and all that day
Had been out on the hills, a perilous way,
But the foot of the deer was far and fleet,
And the wolf kept aloof from the hunter's feet.
And bitter feelings passed o'er him then,
As he stood by the populous haunts of men.

The winds of Autumn came over the woods
As the sun stole out from their solitudes ;
The moss was white on the maple's trunk,
And dead from its arms the pale vine shrunk,
And ripened the mellow fruit hung, and red
Were the tree's withered leaves round it shed.

The foot of the reaper moved slow on the lawn,
And the sickle cut down the yellow corn ;
The mower sung loud by the meadow-side,
Where the mists of evening were spreading wide,
And the voice of the herdsman came up the lea,
And the dance went round by the greenwood tree.

Then the hunter turned away from that scene,
Where the home of his fathers once had been,
And heard by the distant and measured stroke
That the woodman hewed down the giant oak,
And burning thoughts flashed over his mind
Of the white man's faith and love unkind.

The moon of the harvest grew high and bright,
As her golden horn pierced the cloud of white ;
A footstep was heard in the rustling brake
Where the beech overshadowed the misty lake,
And a mourning voice, and a plunge from shore,
And the hunter was seen on the hills no more.

When years had passed on, by that still lakeside
The fisher looked down through the silver tide,
And there, on the smooth, yellow sand displayed,
A skeleton wasted and white was laid,
And 't was seen, as the waters moved deep and slow,
That the hand was still grasping a hunter's bow.

JECKOYVA.

The Indian chief, Jeckoyva, as tradition says, perished alone on the mountain which now bears his name. Night overtook him whilst hunting among the cliffs, and he was not heard of till after a long time, when his half-decayed corpse was found at the foot of a high rock, over which he must have fallen. Mount Jeckoyva is near the White Hills.

THEY made the warrior's grave beside
The dashing of his native tide ;
And there was mourning in the glen —
The strong wail of a thousand men —
   O'er him thus fallen in his pride,
Ere mist of age, or blight, or blast,
Had o'er his mighty spirit past.

•

They made the warrior's grave beneath
The bending of the wild elm's wreath,
When the dark hunter's piercing eye
Had found that mountain rest on high,
   Where, scattered by the sharp wind's breath,
Beneath the rugged cliff were thrown
The strong belt and the mouldering bone.

Where was the warrior's foot, when first
The red sun on the mountain burst ?
Where, when the sultry noontime came
On the green vales with scorching flame,
   And made the woodlands faint with thirst ?
'T was where the wind is keen and loud,
And the gray eagle breasts the cloud.

Where was the warrior's foot when night
Veiled in thick cloud the mountain height ?
None heard the loud and sudden crash,—
None saw the fallen warrior dash
　　Down the bare rock so high and white!
But he that drooped not in the chase
Made on the hills his burial-place.

They found him there, when the long day
Of cold desertion passed away,
And traces on that barren cleft
Of struggling hard with death were left,—
　　Deep marks and footprints in the clay !
And they have laid this feathery helm
By the dark river and green elm.

THE SEA-DIVER.

My way is on the bright blue sea,
　　My sleep upon its rocking tide ;
And many an eye has followed me
　　Where billows clasp the worn seaside.

My plumage bears the crimson blush,
　　When ocean by the sea is kissed ;
When fades the evening's purple flush,
　　My dark wing cleaves the silver mist.

Full many a fathom down beneath
　　The bright arch of the splendid deep

My ear has heard the sea-shell breathe
  O'er living myriads in their sleep.

They rested by the coral throne,
  And by the pearly diadem ;
Where the pale sea-grape had o'ergrown
  The glorious dwellings made for them.

At night upon my storm-drenched wing,
  I poised above a helmless bark,
And soon I saw the shattered thing
  Had passed away and left no mark.

And when the wind and storm were done,
  A ship, that had rode out the gale,
Sunk down, without a signal gun,
  And none was left to tell the tale.

I saw the pomp of day depart,
  The cloud resign its golden crown,
When to the ocean's beating heart
  The sailor's wasted corse went down. .

Peace be to those whose graves are made
  Beneath the bright and silver sea!
Peace, that their relics there were laid
  With no vain pride and pageantry !

MUSINGS.

I sat by my window one night,
  And watch'd how the stars grew high,
And the earth and skies were a splendid sight
  To a sober and musing eye.

From heaven the silver moon shone down
  With gentle and mellow ray,
And beneath the crowded roofs of the town
  In broad light and shadow lay.

A glory was on the silent sea,
  And mainland and island too,
Till a haze came over the lowland lea,
  And shrouded that beautiful blue.

Bright in the moon the autumn wood
  Its crimson scarf unrolled,
And the trees like a splendid army stood
  In a panoply of gold!

I saw them waving their banners high,
  As their crests to the night wind bowed,
And a distant sound on the air went by,
  Like the whispering of a crowd.

Then I watched from my window how fast
  The lights all around me fled,
As the wearied man to his slumber passed,
  And the sick one to his bed.

All faded save one, that burned
  With distant and steady light ;
But that, too, went out, — and I turned
  Where my own lamp within shone bright !

Thus, thought I, our joys must die ;
  Yes, the brightest from earth we win ;
Till each turns away, with a sigh,
  To the lamp that burns brightly within.

SONG.

WHERE, from the eye of day,
  The dark and silent river,
Pursues through tangled woods a way
  O'er which the tall trees quiver, —

The silver mist, that breaks
  From out that woodland cover,
Betrays the hidden path it takes,
  And hangs the current over !

So oft the thoughts that burst
  From hidden springs of feeling,
Like silent streams, unseen at first,
  From our cold hearts are stealing.

But soon the clouds that veil
  The eye of Love, when glowing,
Betray the long unwhispered tale
  Of thoughts in darkness flowing ?

TWO SONNETS FROM THE SPANISH OF FRANCISCO DE MEDRANO.[1]

I.

ART AND NATURE.

Causa la vista el artificio humano, etc.

THE works of human artifice soon tire
  The curious eye ; the fountain's sparkling rill,
  And gardens, when adorned by human skill,
Reproach the feeble hand, the vain desire.
  But oh ! the free and wild magnificence
Of Nature in her lavish hours doth steal,
  In admiration silent and intense,
The soul of him who hath a soul to feel.
  The river moving on its ceaseless way,
The verdant reach of meadows fair and green,
And the blue hills that bound the sylvan scene, —
  These speak of grandeur, that defies decay, —
Proclaim the Eternal Architect on high,
Who stamps on all his works his own eternity.

II.

THE TWO HARVESTS.

Yo vi romper aquestas vegas llanas, etc.

BUT yesterday those few and hoary sheaves
  Waved in the golden harvest ; from the plain
  I saw the blade shoot upward, and the grain

---

[1] These sonnets appeared at the end of Mr. Longellow's first separate publication, "Coplas de Don Jorge Manrique, translated from the Spanish, with an Introductory Essay on the Moral and Devotional Poetry of Spain. By Henry W. Longfellow, Professor of Mod. Lang. and Lit. in Bowdoin College." Boston : Allen and Ticknor, 1833. Pp. 85–87. They have never since been reprinted.

Put forth the unripe ear and tender leaves.
  Then the glad upland smiled upon the view,
And to the air the broad green leaves unrolled,
A peerless emerald in each silken fold,
  And on each palm a pearl of morning dew.
And thus sprang up and ripened in brief space
  All that beneath the reaper's sickle died,
  All that smiled beauteous in the summer-tide.
And what are we ? a copy of that race,
  The later harvest of a longer year !
  And oh ! how many fall before the ripened ear !

No. VI.

[From "The Literary World," Feb. 26, 1882.]

A BIBLIOGRAPHY OF LONGFELLOW.

I.

The Published Works of Mr. Longfellow to Date.

ELEMENTS OF FRENCH GRAMMAR. Translated from the French of C. F. L'Homond. [Boston: 1830.]

ORIGIN AND PROGRESS OF THE FRENCH LANGUAGE. *North Amer. Rev.*, **32**. 277. [April, 1831.]

DEFENCE OF POETRY. *North Am. Rev.*, **34**. 56. [Jan., 1832.]

HISTORY OF THE ITALIAN LANGUAGE AND DIALECTS. *North Am. Rev.*, **35**. 283. [October, 1832.]

SYLLABUS DE LA GRAMMAIRE ITALIENNE. [Boston: 1832.]

COURS DE LANGUE FRANÇAISE. [Boston: 1832.]
　　I. Le Ministre de Wakefield.
　　II. Proverbes Dramatiques.

SAGGI DE' NOVELLIERI ITALIANI D' OGNI SECOLO: Tratti da' più celebri Scrittori, con brevi Notizie intorno alla Vita di ciascheduno. [Boston: 1832.]

SPANISH DEVOTIONAL AND MORAL POETRY. *North Am. Rev.*, **34**. 277. [April, 1832.]

COPLAS DE MANRIQUE. A Translation from the Spanish. [Boston: Allen & Ticknor, 1833.]

Jorge Manrique was a Spanish poet of the fifteenth century. His *Coplas* is a funeral poem on the death of his father, extending to five hundred lines. Mr. Longfellow's volume is prefaced with the above essay on the moral and devotional poetry of Spain, from the *N. A. Rev.*, **34**. 277 ; and included in it are translations of Sonnets by Lope de Vega and others.

Spanish Language and Literature. *North Am. Rev.,* **36.** 316. [April, 1833.]

Old English Romances. *North Am. Rev.,* **37.** 374. [Oct., 1833.]

Outre-Mer; a Pilgrimage beyond the Sea. 2 vols. [New York: Harpers, 1835.]

A series of prose descriptions of foreign travel ; a sort of "Sketchbook." Reviewed by O. W. Peabody in *N. A. Rev.,* **39.** 459–467; in *Am. Month. Rev.,* **4.** 157. Its publication was begun in numbers, by Hilliard, Gray, & Co. [Boston : 1833.]

The Great Metropolis. *North Am. Rev.,* **44.** 461. [April, 1837.]

A lively review of a new work on London.

Hawthorne's Twice Told Tales. *North Am. Rev.,* **45.** 59. [July, 1837.]

Tegnér's Frithiofs Saga. *North Am. Rev.,* **45.** 149. [July, 1837.]

Anglo-Saxon Literature. *North Am. Rev.,* **47.** 90. [July, 1838.]

Hyperion, a Romance. 2 vols. [New York : 1839.]

This was the first of Mr. Longfellow's works written in his Cambridge home, — in the very Washington chamber, indeed, of the Craigie house, where he still resides. Reviewed by C. C. Felton in *N. A. Rev.,* **51.** 145–161 ; in *So. Lit. Mess.,* **5.** 839.

Voices of the Night. [Cambridge: 1839.]

Mr. Longfellow's first volume of poems, containing "The Psalm of Life," "The Reaper and the Flowers," and six other poems, many of which were originally published in the *Knickerbocker Magazine;* also seven "Earlier Poems," as follows, all of which were composed before the author was nineteen: "An April Day," "Autumn," "Woods in Winter," "Hymn of the Moravian Nuns at Bethlehem," "Sunrise on the Hills," "The Spirit of Poetry," "The Burial of the Minnisink."

Reviewed in *N. A. Rev.,* **50.** 266–269 ; *Christ. Ex.,* **28.** 242.

The French Language in England. *North Am. Rev.,* **51.** 285. [Oct., 1840.]

BALLADS AND OTHER POEMS. [Cambridge: 1841.]

Including "The Skeleton in Armor," "The Wreck of the Hesperus," "The Village Blacksmith," "God's Acre," "To the River Charles," and "Excelsior." Reviewed by C. C. Felton in *N. A. Rev.*, **55**. 114–144; by Poe, in his *Literati.*

POEMS ON SLAVERY. [1842.]

Composed during a return voyage from Europe, in 1842.

THE SPANISH STUDENT. A Play in Three Acts. [1843.]

In this dramatic poem may be found the song entitled "Serenade," beginning, "Stars of the summer night." Reviewed in *Lond. Ath.*, 1844, 8; in *Irish Quart. Rev.*, June, 1855, 202; in Poe's *Literati;* in Whipple's *Essays and Reviews*, 1. 66.

[Editor.] THE WAIF: a Collection of Poems. [Cambridge: 1845.]

[Editor.] THE POETS AND POETRY OF EUROPE. [Philadelphia: 1845.]

A collection of selections, translated from a large number of European poets, with introductions and biographical and critical sketches. Many of the translations are by Mr. Longfellow. A new edition, revised and enlarged, was published in 1871. Reviewed by F. Bowen in *N. A. Rev.*, **61**. 199.

THE BELFRY OF BRUGES, and Other Poems. [Boston: 1846.]

[Editor.] THE ESTRAY: a Collection of Poems. [Boston: 1847.]

EVANGELINE: a Tale of Acadie. [Boston: 1847.]

KAVANAGH: a Tale. Prose. [Boston: 1849.]

THE SEASIDE AND THE FIRESIDE. [Boston: 1850.]

Contains "The Building of the Ship," "Resignation," and twenty-one other poems.

THE GOLDEN LEGEND. [Boston: 1851.]

Reviewed in *Blackwood*, **5**. 71; in *Eclec.*, 4th s., **31**. 455.

THE SONG OF HIAWATHA. [Boston: 1855.]

Reviewed by Rev. E. E. Hale in *N. A. Rev.*, **82**. 272.

THE COURTSHIP OF MILES STANDISH. [Boston: 1858.]
With "Birds of Passage, Flight the First," twenty-two poems, including "In the Churchyard at Cambridge" and "The Fiftieth Birthday of Agassiz."
Reviewed by A. P. Peabody in *N. A. Rev.*, **88**. 275.

TALES OF A WAYSIDE INN. [Boston: 1863.]
"First Day," with "Birds of Passage, Flight the Second," seven poems, including "The Children's Hour," and "The Cumberland."

FLOWER-DE-LUCE. [Boston: 1867.]
Twelve poems.

NEW ENGLAND TRAGEDIES. [Boston: 1868.]
I. John Endicott.
II. Giles Cory of the Salem Farms.
Reviewed by E. J. Cutler in *N. A. Rev.*, **108**. 669.

DANTE'S DIVINE COMEDY. A Translation. [Boston: 1867–70.]
Three vols. I. Inferno. II. Purgatorio. III. Paradiso. The same in 1 vol.
Reviewed by Charles Eliot Norton in *N. A. Rev.*, **105**. 125; by George W. Greene in *Atlantic M.*, **20**. 188.

THE DIVINE TRAGEDY. [Boston: 1872.]
CHRISTUS: A MYSTERY. [Boston: 1872.]
Collecting, for the first time, into their consecutive unity :—
I. The Divine Tragedy.
II. The Golden Legend.
III. The New England Tragedies.

THREE BOOKS OF SONG. [Boston: 1872.]
Contents: "Tales of a Wayside Inn, Second Day"; "Judas Maccabæus (a dramatic poem in five acts); and "A Handful of Translations," eleven in number.

AFTERMATH. [Boston: 1874.]
Contents: "Tales of a Wayside Inn, Third Day," and "Birds of Passage, Flight the Third."

The Masque of Pandora, and Other Poems.   [Boston: 1875.]

Contents: "The Hanging of the Crane"; "Morituri Salutamus," the Bowdoin College poem for the semi-centennial of the author's class of 1825; "Birds of Passage, Flight the Fourth"; and "A Book of Sonnets," fourteen in all. (An operatic version of "The Masque of Pandora" was produced on the Boston stage in January, 1881.)

[Editor.] Poems of Places. **31** vols. [Boston: 1876–1879.]

Kéramos; and Other Poems. [Boston: 1878.]

Contents: A "Fifth Flight" of "Birds of Passage," sixteen in all, among which are the tribute to James Russell Lowell entitled "The Herons of Elmwood," and "The White Czar"; a second "Book of Sonnets," nineteen of them, including "The Three Silences," the *Literary World* tribute to Whittier, "The Two Rivers," and "St. John's, Cambridge"; and fifteen translations, eight from Michael Angelo.

Ultima Thule. [Boston: 1880.]

II.

Additional Notices of Mr. Longfellow.

Arnaud, Simon. *La Légende Dorée.* [In *Le Correspondant*, 10 Juillet, 1872.]

Cobb, J. B.   Miscellanies. [1858.] pp. 330–357.

Curtis, G. W. *Atlantic Monthly.* **12.** 269.

Mr. Curtis's "Easy Chair" in Harper's Monthly contains notices of Mr. Longfellow and his writings, as follows: "The Dante," **35.** 257; "Reception in England," **37.** 561; "New England Tragedies," **38.** 271; "The Divine Tragedy," **44.** 616. There is also a general article on Longfellow in **1.** 74.

Cochin, Augustin. *La Poésie en Amérique.* [In *Le Correspondant*, 10 Juillet, 1872.]

DEPRET, Louis. *Le Va-et-Vient.* [Paris : n. d.]

The same. *La Poésie en Amérique.* [Lille : 1876.]

DE PRINS, A. *Études Américaines.* [Louvain : 1877.]

FRISWELL, J. H. *Modern Men of Letters.* [1870.] pp. 285–299.

GILFILLAN, George. *Literary Portraits.* Second Series.

PALMER, Ray. Longfellow and his Works. *Int. Rev.,* Nov., 1875.

PECK, G. W. Review of Mr. Longfellow's *Evangeline.* [New York : 1848.]

P. T. C. *Kalevala and Hiawatha.* A Review. [185–.] pp. 21.

WHIPPLE, E. P. *Essays and Reviews.* 1. 60–63.

III.

Translations of Mr. Longfellow's Works.

ENGLISH.

NoËL. [A French poem by Longfellow in *Flower-de-Luce.*] Tr. by J. E. Norcross. [Philadelphia : 1867. Large paper. 50 copies printed.]

GERMAN.

Englische Gedichte aus Neuerer Zeit. Freiligrath, Ferdinand. . . . H. W. Longfellow . . . [Stuttgart und Tübingen : 1846.]

Longfellow's Gedichte. Übersetzt von Carl Böttger. [Dessau : 1856.]

Balladen und Lieder von H. W. Longfellow. Deutsch von A. R. Nielo. [Münster : 1857.]

Longfellow's Gedichte. Von Friedrich Marx. [Hamburg and Leipzig : 1868.]

Longfellow's aeltere und neuere Gedichte in Auswald. Deutsch von Adolf Laun. [Oldenburg: 1879.]

Der Spanische Studente. Übersetzt von Karl Böttger. [Dessau: 1854.]

The Same. Von Maria Helene Le Maistre. [Dresden: n. d.]

The Same. Übersetzt von Häfeli. [Leipzig: n. d.]

Evangeline. Aus dem Englischen. [Hamburg: 1857.]

The Same. Aus dem Englischen, von P. J. Belke. [Leipzig: 1854.]

The Same. Eine Erzählung aus Acadien. Von Eduard Nickles. [Karlsruhe: 1862.]

The Same. Übersetzt von Frank Siller. [Milwaukee: 1879.]

The Same. Übersetzt von Karl Knortz. [Leipzig: n. d.]

Longfellow's Evangeline. Deutsch von Heinrich Viehoff. [Trier: 1869.]

Die Goldene Legende. Deutsch von Karl Keck. [Wien: 1859.]

The Same. Übersetzt von Elise Freifrau von Hohenhausen. [Leipzig: 1880.]

Das Lied von Hiawatha. Deutsch von Adolph Böttger. [Leipzig: 1856.]

Der Sang von Hiawatha. Übersetzt von Ferdinand Freiligrath. [Stuttgart und Augsburg: 1857.]

Hiawatha. Übertragen von Hermann Simon. [Leipzig: n. d.]

Der Sang von Hiawatha. Übersetzt, eingeleitet und erklärt von Karl Knortz. [Jena: 1872.]

Miles Standish's Brautwerbung. Aus dem Englischen von F. E. Baumgarten. [St. Louis: 1859.]

Die Brautwerbung des Miles Standish. Übersetzt von Karl Knortz. [Leipzig: 18—.]

Miles Standish's Brautwerbung. Übersetzt von F. Manefeld. [1867.]

Die Sage von König Olaf. Übersetzt von Ernst Rauscher.

The Same. Übersetzt von W. Hertzberg.

Dorfschmid. Die Alte Uhr auf der Treppe. Des Schlaven Traum. Tr. by H. Schmick. *Archiv. f. d. Stud. d. n. Spr.,* 1858, **24**. 214–217.

Gedichte von H. W. L. Deutsch von Alexander Neidhardt. [Darmstadt: 1856.]

Der Bau des Schiffes. Tr. by Th. Zermelo. *Archiv. f. d. Stud. d. n. Spr.,* 1861, **30**. 293–304.

Hyperion. Deutsch von Adolph Böttger. [Leipzig: 1856.]

Ein Psalm des Lebens, etc. Deutsch von Alexander Neidhardt. *Archiv. f. d. Stud. d. n. Spr.,* 1856, **29**. 205–208.

Die Göttliche Tragödie. Übersetzt von Karl Keck. [MS.]

The Same. Übersetzt von Hermann Simon. [MS.]

Pandora. Übersetzt von Isabella Schuchardt. [Hamburg: 1878.]

Morituri Salutamus. Übersetzt von Dr. Ernst Schmidt. [Chicago: 1878.]

The Hanging of the Crane. Das Kesselhängen. Übersetzt von G. A. Zündt. [n. d.]

The Same. Das Einhängen des Kesselhakens, frei gearbeitet von Joh. Henry Becker. [n. d.]

DUTCH.

Het Lied van Hiawatha. In het Nederdeutsch overgebragt door L. S. P. Meijboom. [Amsterdam: 1862.]

Miles Standish. Nagezongen door S. I. Van den Berg. Haarlem: 1861.]

SWEDISH.

Hyperion. På Svenska, af Grönlund. [1853.]

Evangeline. På Svenska, af Alb. Lysander. [1854.]

The Same. Öfversatt af Hjalmar Erdgren. [Göteborg: 1875.]
The Same. Öfversatt af Philip Svenson. [Chicago: 1875.]
Hiawatha. På Svenska af Westberg. [1856.]

DANISH.

Evangeline. Paa Norsk ved Sd. C. Knutsen. [Christiania: 1874.]
Sangen om Hiawatha. Oversat af G. Bern. [Kjöbenhavn: 1860.]

FRENCH.

Evangeline ; suivie des Voix de la Nuit. Par le Chevalier de Chatelain. [Jersey, London, Paris, New York: 1856.]
The Same. Conte d'Acadie. Traduit par Charles Brunel. Prose. [Paris: 1864.]
The Same. Par Léon Pamphile Le May. [Quebec: 1865.]
La Légende Dorée, et Poëmes sur l'Esclavage. Traduits par Paul Blier et Edward Mac-Donnel. Prose. [Paris et Valenciennes: 1854.]
Hiawatha. Traduit de l'Anglais par M. H. Gomont. [Nancy, Paris: 1860.]
Drames et Poésies. Traduits par X. Marmier. The New England Tragedies. [Paris: 1872.]
Hyperion et Kavanagh. Traduit de l'Anglais, et précédé d'une Notice sur l'Auteur. 2 vols. [Paris et Bruxelles: 1860.]
The Psalm of Life, and Other Poems. Tr. by Lucien de la Rive in *Essais de Traduction Poétique.* [Paris: 1870.]

ITALIAN.

Alcune Poesie di Enrico W. Longfellow. Traduzione dall' Inglese di Angelo Messedaglia. [Padova: 1866.]

Lo Studente Spagnuolo. Prima Versione Metrica di Messandro Bazzini. [Milano: 1871.]

The Same. Traduzione di Nazzareno Trovanèlli. [Firenze: 1876.]

Poesie sulla Schiavitù. Tr. in Versi Italiani da Louisa Grace Bartolini. [Firenze: 1860.]

Evangelina. Tradotta da Pietro Rotondi. [Firenze: 1857.]

The Same. Traduzione di Carlo Faccioli. [Verona: 1873.]

La Leggenda d' Oro. Tradotta da Ada Corbellini Martini. [Parma: 1867.]

Il Canto d' Hiawatha. Tr. da L. G. Bartolini. Frammenti. [Firenze: 1867.]

Miles Standish. Traduzione dall' Inglese di Caterino Frattini. [Padova: 1868.]

PORTUGUESE.

El Rei Roberto de Sicilia. Tr. by Dom Pedro II., Emperor of Brazil. [Autograph MS.]

Evangelina. Traducida por Franklin Doria. [Rio de Janeiro: 1874.]

The Same. Poema de Henrique Longfellow. Traducido por Miguel Street de Arriaga. [Lisbon: n. d.]

The Same. By Flavio Reimar, in the *Aurora Brasileira,* 1874; and by José de Goes Filho, in the *Municipio,* 1874.

SPANISH.

Evangelina. Romance de la Acadia. Traducido del Ingles por Carlos Mórla Vicuña. [Nueva York: 1871.]

POLISH.

Zlota Legenda. The Golden Legend. Tr. into Polish by F. Jerzierski. [Warszawa: 1857.]

23

Evangelina.   Tr. into Polish by Felix Jerzierski.   [Warszawa: 1857.]

Duma o Hiawacie.   The Song of Hiawatha.   Tr. into Polish by Feliksa Jerzierskiego.   [Warszawa: 1860.]

RUSSIAN AND OTHER LANGUAGES.

Excelsior, and Other Poems, in Russian.   [St. Petersburg: n. d.]

Hiawatha, rendered into Latin, with abridgment.   By Francis William Newman.   [London: 1862.]

Excelsior.   Tr. into Hebrew by Henry Gersoni.   [n. d.]

A Psalm of Life.   In Marathi.   By Mrs. H. I. Bruce.   [Satara: 1878.]

The Same.   In Chinese.   By Jung Tagen.   [Written on a fan.]

The Same.   In Sanscrit.   By Elihu Burritt and his pupils.

The sales of Longfellow's works up to 1857 are thus given by Allibone in his *Dictionary of Authors:*—

Title.	Date of Publication.	Copies.
Voices of the Night	1839	43,000
Ballads and Other Poems	1841	40,000
The Spanish Student	1843	38,000
The Belfry of Bruges	1846	38,000
Evangeline	1847	37,000
The Seaside and the Fireside	1849	30,000
The Golden Legend	1851	17,000
Hiawatha	1855	50,000
Outre-Mer	1835	7,500
Hyperion	1839	14,550
Kavanagh	1849	10,500
Total		325,550

Of Longfellow's collected works in four of the leading editions, there have been printed to date as follows : —

Edition.	*Date of Publication.*	*Copies.*
Diamond	1867	110,000
Red Line	1869	20,500
Household	1873	57,500
Library	1876	6,000
Total		194,000

University Press : John Wilson & Son, Cambridge.